WHAT THE DEAD MEN SAY

AN EVANS NOVEL OF THE WEST

WHAT THE DEAD MEN SAY

EDWARD GORMAN

M. EVANS & COMPANY, INC. NEW YORK

Library of Congress Cataloging-in-Publication Data

Gorman, Edward.

   What The Dead Men Say / Edward Gorman.
     p.   cm.—(An Evans novel of the West)
   ISBN 0-87131-614-5
   I. Title.   II. Series.
PS3557.0759W47   1989   90-37050
813'.54—dc20   CIP

Copyright © 1990 by Edward Gorman

M. Evans and Company, Inc.
216 East 49 Street
New York, New York 10017

Manufactured in the United States of America

9 8 7 6 5 4 3 2 1

This is for my friend and colleague
Wayne Dundee

The title of this novel is taken from a short story by Philip K. Dick. I felt it was appropriate here.

E.G.

I used John Madson's excellent *Stories From Under the Sky* (Iowa State University Press) as background in two scenes. If you're interested in nature lore, you'll like Madson's book as much as I do.

E.G.

The newspaper account told it this way:

On the sunny morning of June 27, 1898 a thirteen-year-old girl named Clarice Ryan walked into the First Trust Bank of Council Bluffs, Iowa.

Out of school for the summer, Clarice was helping her father Septemus, one of the town's leading merchants, by taking the morning deposit to the bank.

Ordinarily, Clarice always stopped by the office of bank president Charles Dolan. The banker is said to have kept a drawerful of mints for the express purpose of giving one to his "lady friend," Clarice, each working morning.

On this particular morning, however, Clarice was unable to visit her friend Dolan. As soon as she walked into the bank, she saw immediately that a robbery was in progress.

Against the east wall, four customers stood with their hands up as a man with a red bandana over his face held a shotgun on them. His two companions, one wearing a blue bandana, the other wearing a green one, stood near the safe while two clerks and Mr. Charles Dolan himself emptied greenbacks into three sailcloth bags.

The man in the blue bandana ordered Clarice to stand over next to the other customers. Like them, she was told to put her hands over her head. Witnesses said the young girl smiled when she was told this. Scared as she was, she obviously found the order to be a little silly.

When all the greenbacks had been taken from the safe, the three thieves gathered in the middle of the bank. At this point Dolan and the two clerks were moved over to join Clarice and the other customers.

It was then that policeman Michael Walden, who had seen what was going on from the window on the boardwalk outside, came through the door with his own shotgun, ordering the men to lay down their arms.

The rest of the story remains confused, Deputy Walden insisting that he fired only because one of the thieves opened fire on him. Two of the customers insisted that it was Walden who fired first.

At some point in the minute-long exchange of gunfire, one of the adult customers was shot in the shoulder. One of the thieves was also wounded, though all three managed to escape. Clarice Ryan, shot in the heart, was killed instantly.

Several rewards have been offered for the capture of the thieves. "I guess I don't need to say dead or alive," Council Bluffs Police Chief Dennis Foster told assembled reporters. "And a lot of folks would just as soon see them slung over horses and brought in dead as otherwise."

Investigation into the death of thirteen-year-old Clarice Ryan continues.

Chapter One

1

From the second-floor hotel veranda he could look down into the dusty street and see the women twirling their parasols and hurrying about in their bustles. These were town women with sweet Christian faces and sweet Christian souls. Carlyle, six years out of prison at Fort Madison, wanted such a woman. He imagined that their juices were tastier, their love by turns gentler and wilder, and their soft words in the darkness afterward balming like a cool breeze on a hot July afternoon. He would never know. Sweet Christian women had never taken to Carlyle. He had put his seed only in whores and long ago his seed had turned to poison.

Right now, though, Carlyle wasn't worrying about women, sweet or otherwise. He was looking at the two riders who were coming down the middle of the street, one astride a roan, one on a dun. A water wagon followed them, cutting the dust with sprays of silver water. Behind the wagon ran some noisy town kids waving and jumping and laughing and carrying on the way kids always did when they were three days out of school and just beginning summer vacation.

The two riders didn't seem to notice the kids. They didn't seem to notice much, in fact. The small midwestern town was a showcase hereabouts, what with electricity, telephones, and a depot that President Harrison himself had once told the local Odd Fellows club was "most singularly impressive." Anyone could tell, therefore, that the two riders came from a city. Country folks always gawked when they came to Myles. City folks, who'd seen it all already, were too cynical and spoiled to gawk.

One of the riders was a boy, probably sixteen or so, tall and lanky, with a handsome rugged face. But it was on the other rider that Carlyle settled his attention. The man was short, somewhat chunky, packed into a dark vested suit far too hot for an afternoon like this. He wore a derby and carried a Winchester in his scabbard.

Carlyle knew the man. Oh, didn't know him in the sense that they'd spoken or anything, but knew him in the sense that the man was in some way familiar.

Carlyle raised his beer mug and sipped from it just as, sprawled in a chair behind him, the whore yawned again. She was too wide and too white. It was for the latter reason that she liked to sit out on the veranda, so the sun would tan her arms and bare legs. In her petticoats she was damned near naked and it seemed she could care less. Her name was Jenna and she and Carlyle had been living in the same hotel room for the past eight months. Last night she'd started talking marriage again and Carlyle, just drunk enough and not impressed by her threats of leaving him if he ever slapped her again, doubled his fist and poked it once straight and hard into her eye. Her shiner this morning was a beauty. Of course, he'd had to offer her something in compensation. Not marriage, he said; but teeth. Store-bought teeth. Hers were little brown stubs that made her mouth smell so bad he had to down two buckets of beer before he could bring himself to kiss her.

"What the hell you lookin' at so hard?" Jenna wanted to know.

"Man."

"What man?"

"Man on a dun."

"You never saw a man on no dun before?"

"Wonder why he came here."

"Came where?"

"To town. Myles."

"Free country."

"Yeah, but he wants somethin' special."

"How you know that?"

"You can see by the way he rides. Like he's just waitin' for somethin' to happen."

"That's how I was last night," Jenna laughed. "Waitin' for somethin' to happen."

He looked back at her. "You don't like it, you whore, you can always move out."

"Just a joke, Henry. Jus' teasin'. Too much beer affects most men that way."

But Carlyle was no longer listening. He had turned his attention back to the street and the two riders. Halfway down the block, and across the street, they were dismounting in front of the McAlester Hotel. Unlike the place where Carlyle and the whore lived, the McAlester didn't have cockroaches and colored maids who went through your room trying to steal stuff.

"Sonofabitch," Carlyle said.

"What?"

"I just recognized who he is."

"Who is he?"

"Sonofabitch," Carlyle said again.

He went back to the whore and tried to hand her his beer mug.

"I don't want that thing. I ain't your maid," she said. She could get real bitchy, this one.

Carlyle threw the beer in her face.

"You ain't got no right to do that," she said, spitting out suds.

"Hell if I don't," Carlyle said. "Long as I pay the rent on that room, I got a right to do any god damn thing I please."

Then he was gone, inside to his room and then into the hallway and then down the stairs to the lobby. He took two steps at a time.

He had suddenly remembered, from all the pictures in the newspapers right after it happened, who the man was.

He did not stop hurrying until he was two blocks from the downtown area, and running down a side street so fast people stopped to look at him.

2

The kid's name was James Patrick George Hogan, George being his confirmation name, taken for the saint who slew dragons. In his Catholic school book there had been an illustration of George in armor and mail standing triumphant with his huge battle sword near a slain dragon. The dragon's scales and reptilian snout had captivated James.

Looking at illustrations of dragons and dinosaurs was his favorite pastime. He could stare at them for hours, imagining himself living back then. The only thing wrong with this was that back then there would have been no Marietta Courtney, this being the fourteen-year-old public-school girl James had been steadfastly stuck on since he'd seen her a year ago riding her bicycle, her red hair gorgeous in the sunlight, her smile in equal parts impish and unknowable.

These were some of the things James had thought about on the last part of the journey to Myles. His uncle Septemus Ryan had fallen into one of his silences. Of course, James knew what the silence was about: a few years back his uncle's girl—and James's favorite cousin—Clarice, had been shot and killed in a bank robbery back in their hometown. This had been particularly hard on Septemus, because only two years previously his wife had died from whooping cough.

Since these deaths there had been a lot of talk in Council Bluffs about "poor Septemus not being quite right upstairs." He was given to violent tempers, unending days and nights of brooding, and talking to himself. The latter seemed particularly troubling to Council Bluffians. Here was a leading merchant, and a darned handsome one at that, walking down the streets of town quite obviously carrying on some kind of conversation with himself. What he was saying or to whom was a mystery, of course, and a disturbing one to those who cared about him.

In the dusty street, James and Septemus dismounted. They took the carpetbags from their saddles and carried them inside the hotel.

James appreciated the cooling shade of the fine hotel lobby. Gentlemen in percale shirts and straw boaters and cheery red sleeve garters sat in leather chairs smoking cigars, sipping lemonade, and reading newspapers and magazines. A few yellowbacks were even in evidence. James wondered if any of them were reading *The Train Boy,* which next to the works of Sir Walter Scott was the best thing he'd ever read.

The lobby had mahogany wainscoting and genuine brass cuspidors and great green ferns. The mustached man behind the registration desk looked as snappy as a man in a Sears catalog.

"Good afternoon, sir," the clerk said in a splendid manly voice.

"Afternoon," Septemus said. "One room, two beds. And we'll be wanting baths this afternoon."

"Cool ones, I trust, sir," the clerk said, smiling.

Septemus didn't smile back. The clerk, something dying in his eyes, looked mortally offended.

Up in their room, they emptied the carpetbags on their beds and then sat in the two chairs next to the window to sip their complimentary lemonade.

"You glad you came along?" Septemus said. Here it was three degrees hotter than down on the street, but here they could feel the breeze better, too. Septemus had taken his jacket and his vest off. At forty-five he was balding and getting fat, but he still looked muscular and his hard, angular face attracted women and made men wary. He didn't look at all like a haberdasher.

"Yessir."

"There you go again."

James blushed. "I'm sorry."

"No need to apologize, James. You've just got to remember the things I'm trying to teach you."

James nodded.

"You know why I took you on this trip?"."

"Because you wanted to take me to the state fair." The fair was in Des Moines, some one hundred miles away. There would be amusement rides and prize livestock and bearded ladies and magicians and probably two hundred girls who were as cute as Marietta Courtney. Or at least James hoped so.

"The fair is part of the reason but it's not all of the reason."

"It's not?"

Septemus looked at James very hard. "I wanted to get you away from your mother's influence."

"You did?"

"I did."

"You don't like my mom?"

"I like your mom fine but she's not the best influence you could have."

"She's not?"

"Nope. Your father was."

"But he is dead."

"I'm well aware of that."

"And my mom has done a good job of raisin' us three kids ever since."

Septemus still looked solemn. "Your mother is my sister and a woman I respect no end. But she's a lot better mother to your two sisters than she is to you."

"She is?"

Septemus nodded, then sipped some lemonade. "Think about it, James."

"About what?"

"About what your life has been like since your father died. Without a proper male influence, that is."

"I don't understand."

"Violin lessons. Always wearing knickers and a clean dress shirt. Spending most of your time on studies instead of being outside playing baseball. Do you honestly think this is a natural state of affairs for any young man? And that's what you are, James, whether your mother chooses to acknowledge it or not. You're sixteen and that makes you a young man."

"I guess I never thought of it that way."

"When your father was your age, he was supporting a family of three and going to work for the Union Central Life Insurance Company. By the time he was twenty, he had his own office."

"That's right, Uncle Septemus."

"And he was a man known to take a drink who could hold a drink, and a man known to hunt who had respect for the rifle and the prey alike, and a man known to please the ladies just by the manliness of his stride and the confidence of his smile. He was one hell of a real man."

James couldn't help it. Hearing his father recalled so lovingly—Septemus and James's father had been best friends for many years—James got tears in his eyes and had a hard time swallowing.

"Your father wouldn't have approved of the violin lessons. Or the musicals in your parlor every Tuesday night. Or all those luncheons your mother takes you to."

"He wouldn't have?"

Septemus shook his head. "No, he wouldn't have. And that's why I brought you along on this trip."

James looked perplexed.

"To start teaching you about manly things," Septemus said. "Away from the influence of your mother."

"Oh."

"So stop being so deferential. Stop always 'Yessiring' me. A gentlemen is always polite, but that doesn't mean he has to be bowing and scraping. You understand that?"

James almost said "Yessir." Instead, he caught himself on time and simply nodded.

"Good. Now why don't you take a bath. I've got to go do a little business. I'll be back to take my own bath and then we can get something to eat."

Septemus got up and stood over James and mussed his hair with thick fingers. "You look more like your father all the time. You should be proud of that."

"I am."

For the first time since they'd left Council Bluffs, Septemus smiled. "This trip'll be good for you, James. You wait and see."

Then, his boots loud on the linoleum floor in the drowsy quiet of the afternoon, he went over and put his vest and coat back on.

James couldn't help but notice that Septemus also picked up his Winchester.

"See you in an hour or so, James," Septemus said.

Then he was gone.

3

Golden dust motes rolled in the sunlight angling through a hat-sized hole in the roof of the barn. Griff was always meaning to fix it but that would happen only if the Rochester Wagon Works opened its doors again and rehired the eighty-six men they had laid off four and a half years ago. Griff was a big man, blond and open, and in the old days had always been laughing. He had a wife who'd loved him since they'd been kids on adjoining farms, and two little girls who never seemed to tire of running up to him with their arms spread wide, having him pick them up and pretend he was dancing with them.

But one day Mr. Rochester himself had come to the plant and said, with genuine dismay, "Men, the bank won't loan me no more money and our bills are just too far backed up; I'm gonna have to lay you all off. I'm sorry, men." There had been real tears in Mr. Rochester's eyes, and the men knew the tears were not fake because Mr. Rochester was just like them, a workingman who'd got lucky with his invention for building surreys a certain way, and who then, like most workingmen, got unlucky, too. He knew a hell of a lot about surreys, did Mr. Rochester, but he didn't know a damn about money; his pride and fear were such that he wouldn't listen to anybody either, even the well-intentioned bankers who'd meant to help him. So he'd gone bust with a bad hand, and his eighty-odd employees had gone bust right along with him.

There followed those events that always seem to follow men losing good jobs. Drink turned some of them mean and they beat their loving wives, and some even beat their children. At workingmen's taverns blood spilled all the time now, not just during the occasional Saturday brawl. The best of the men, the ones who didn't turn to drink and violence, tried to get other jobs; but, prosperous as the town was, there were no other jobs, not good ones anyway, not ones that could replace what they'd earned (and the kind of self-esteem they'd felt) as employees of the Rochester Wagon Works. These men took to serving the gentry, for there was a large class of rich people in the town. They became gardeners and handymen and drivers and housepainters; they learned how to say yes ma'm and yessir so sweet you almost couldn't hear the contempt in their voices for the spoiled, pushy, inconsiderate rich folks who employed them. They had no choice. They had families to feed.

It was sometime during this period when the happy Griff became the sorrowful Griff. He worked half a dozen jobs that first year after Rochester closed down, the worst of them being as a helper to one of the town's three morticians. He had hated seeing how the blood ran in the gutters of the undertaker's table and he had hated the white fishbelly look to the flesh of corpses and most especially the high fetid smell of the dead that he could never quite get clean of his nostrils. He tried getting back to farming somehow, but this was a time of many bank failures in the midwest, currency shaky as hell, and so he could find nobody to stake him.

It was then that he evolved the idea of robbing banks. It would be simple enough. He would take two of the men he had worked with at Rochester—Kittredge, because he had good nerves and was intelligent; Carlyle, because he had the kind of Saturday night beery courage you needed in tight spots—and together they would travel in a three-hundred-mile semicircular radius (he had this drawn out on a map) and hold up banks three times a year. Kittredge and Carlyle were happy to be invited in. They had agreed to two inviolate propositions: Griff had the final say in any dispute, and there was to be no violence. No violence whatsoever. It was in the course of their very first robbery that either Kittredge or Carlyle (Griff could never be sure) panicked and the little girl got killed. It had been purely an accident—my God, nobody would shoot a little girl—but that didn't make her any less dead. The three men had been so sickened by the sight of the little girl lying in blood and dead on the floor that they forgot to grab the money. They left with guns blazing, empty-handed. They were lucky to escape.

So now he stood in the dusty sunlight of the long July afternoon in a barn that smelled of wood and tarpaper and hay and dogshit from the girls' collie. It smelled most especially of the grease and oil he used to work on his top grade surrey, the one expensive thing he'd ever bought in his forty-one years, bought at a forty-percent employee discount from Rochester back in the good working days. The surrey was fringed and built on elliptic end springs, and had axles of fifteen-sixteenths of an inch, wheels of seven-eighths of an inch and quarter-inch steel tires. The gear was made of second-growth timber ironed with genuine Norway iron and the upholstery was Evans leather. How nice it had been to take this spanking new surrey out for a Sunday drive behind a powerful dun, the girls sitting between Griff and his wife, the neighbors smiling and waving. Down Main Street they'd go every sunny Sunday, church done and a beef roast on the stove, past the Southern Hotel and the big stone bank building, the telegraph office and the telephone office, and McDougall the dentist's. Even a workingman could feel respectable in such circumstances.

Griff was just oiling the axle when he heard the collie, standing in the sunlight just outside the shade of the barn, start to bark. He looked over his shoulder and saw Carlyle. Carlyle looked upset. He also looked drunk. Ever since the little girl had died, Carlyle had spent most of his time on whores and whiskey. Griff no longer liked the man. "Told you I'd just as soon not have you come on my property."

"Don't give a good god damn what you told me."

Griff put down the oil can and turned around. He made fists of his hands. Because he was big and blond and fair, most people mistook him for a Swede, but he was Irish and had an Irish temper. "Don't appreciate you talking to me that way on my own property."

Carlyle didn't seem to hear. "He's here."

"Who's here?"

"Right in town."

Griff could see that Carlyle was caught up in his fear and his drunkenness. He reached out and took the gawky man by the shoulder. Carlyle smelled of sweat and heat and soured beer. Griff turned his face away as he said, "I want you to get hold of yourself."

"I got hold of myself."

"No, you don't."

"I'm tryin' to tell you, Griff, he's god damn here."

"And I'm tryin' to ask you, Carlyle, who's god damn here."

"Her father."

"Whose father?"

"The little girl's."

"Jesus Christ," Griff said. He almost never took the Lord's name in vain. To him that was a significant sin—even a mortal sin that had to be confessed as such to Father Malloy—but right now he didn't care. "How do you know it's him?"

"We've seen his picture, ain't we, a hunnerd times."

"You're sure?"

"Griff, I'm positive."

"Maybe it's just a coincidence."

"Could be, but I doubt it."

Griff wiped sweat from his brow with his forearm. "How the hell could he have found us?"

"Maybe he never quit lookin'."

Griff came out from the cool shadows of the barn to stand in the sunlight with Carlyle. Carlyle looked old now. He had a couple of days' worth of beard and some of his hairs were black and some of them were white. His nose was kind of running and he hadn't cleaned the morning dirt from the corners of his eyes.

"What we gonna do?" Carlyle said.

"Nothing we can do. Not right now. Not till we see what he wants."

"Oh, I can tell you quick and proper what he wants, Griff."

"And what would that be?" Griff said. He felt calmer now, more in control of himself, the way he usually did.

"He wants us dead. All three of us."

"Can you blame him? We killed his little girl."

"Not on purpose."

"That don't bring her back to life."

Carlyle looked as if he were about to cry. "What the hell we gonna do, Griff? You're supposed to be the boss. You tell me."

"You go back to the hotel and relax."

"Yeah, sure, Griff. I sure can relax knowin' some sonofabitch is lookin' for me."

"Get ahold of Kittredge."

"And tell him what?"

"Tell him to meet us at nine tonight at the west end of the Second Avenue bridge."

"You know what he's like, Griff. He won't be able to handle this."

Griff stared at him hard. "He won't have much choice, Carlyle. None of us do." He nodded to the street. "Now go tell him and then stay in your room till you go to the bridge."

"You sure like givin' orders, don't you?"

Griff smiled without much humor. "If you want me to play boss then you better get used to me givin' orders. You understand me?"

Carlyle looked sulky. "I don't like none of this."

"Get going. And get going *now*."

Carlyle shook his head, wiped some sweat from his face, and then set off down the driveway to the street.

Griff watched the man go. Then his girls came up and jumped up and down around him in their faded gingham dresses. If good times ever rolled around again, the first thing Griff planned to do was buy the girls some new clothes. Now they wore hand-me-downs from in-laws and Griff, a proud man, just hated to see it.

Kneeling on his haunches, he drew the two girls close to him and hugged them tight with his eyes closed.

"Boy, it sure is hot, Daddy," Eloise said.

"It sure is," Tess agreed.

But that was the funny thing to Griff. Hot as it was—the afternoon ablaze now at three o'clock—he felt so cold he was shivering.

He hugged the girls even tighter, and tried not to think of how the little girl in the bank had looked that morning, bloody and dead on the linoleum floor.

Chapter Two

1

Just off the sidewalk there was a huge oak, one with roots like claws, and beneath it stood Ryan. On so hot a day he appreciated the shade, though curiously he left his vest and suitcoat on. Hanging loose from his left hand was his Winchester.

For the past ten minutes, Ryan had kept his brown eyes fixed on the small, white cottagelike house and the large barn that loomed over it directly behind. Griff and Carlyle were back there now, talking.

Ryan set the Winchester against the tree then took out a cigar and lighted it. Even on a day this hot, the fifty-cent Cuban tasted good, heady as wine the first few puffs.

A small boy pulling a small red wooden wagon inside of which sat an even smaller girl came by, followed by a yipping puppy. Ryan said hello to the boy and smiled at the puppy. The girl, even though she said hello, received nothing from Ryan, not even a glance. He knew better than to look at pretty girls.

As the kids and the wagon and the dog rolled past, Ryan looked down the street and saw Carlyle coming up the walk, moving fast. He looked agitated.

Carlyle didn't seem to see Ryan until he was a few feet from the tree.

Ryan hefted the Winchester then stepped out into the middle of the walk.

Carlyle, sensing rather than seeing somebody moving into his way, stopped abruptly and raised his head. "Shit," he said when he saw who it was.

"Kind of a hot day to be moving so fast, Mr. Carlyle," Ryan said.

Carlyle's eyes had dropped to the new Winchester slung across Ryan's chest.

Ryan said, "You know who I am, don't you?"

"Yessir."

"And you know why I'm here."

"Yessir."

Ryan patted the Winchester. "And you know why I brought this."

Carlyle said, "It was an accident, sir, what happened to your daughter."

"You know, I've tried to console myself with that notion every once in a while. But then I start to thinking—if those three men hadn't gone to the bank that day, then the accident would never have happened. My little Clarice would have gone in there and made her deposit and Mr. Dolan would have given her a mint and then she would have walked back to my store and it would have been a regular, normal day." Now the tears came, but more in his voice than in his eyes. "She would have graduated from school this past spring, Mr. Carlyle. Her mother and I would have been so proud."

"We didn't mean for it to happen, Mr. Ryan. Honest."

"You know what happened to her mother?"

"No."

Ryan drew himself up and sighed. "Whooping cough."

Carlyle's eyes dropped back to the Winchester.

Ryan said, "You can always go to the sheriff here, Mr. Carlyle."

"Yessir."

"You can always tell him you were the men who robbed that bank and killed that little girl."

"Yessir."

"Because if you don't—" Now it was Ryan who looked at the Winchester. "Because if you don't, you're going to have to worry about me."

"Yessir."

"And you know something?"

"What, sir?"

"I'd sure as hell rather have to worry about the law than worry about me. Because maybe in a court of law you'll convince a jury that what you did was an accident—but you'll never convince me. You understand that?"

Carlyle didn't even have time to respond before Ryan raised the Winchester and slammed the butt of it into Carlyle's mouth.

Carlyle moaned, putting his hands to his mouth. He sounded as if he didn't know whether to puke or cry or what.

Ryan said. "That's just the start of things, Mr. Carlyle. Just the beginning."

But Carlyle wasn't paying any attention. He was looking at the tiny white stubs of teeth he'd just spit out bloodily into the palm of his right hand. He looked shocked and confused and terrified.

"Just the beginning," Ryan said, and walked off down the street toward town again.

James Hogan lay on his bed thinking of what he was going to say to his uncle Septemus as soon as he saw him. Septemus had no right to speak so slightingly of either James or his mother. She'd done a good job of raising all the kids and if she wasn't quite as good a father as she'd been a mother, well, you still couldn't blame her because she was a refined lady whose tastes just naturally gravitated to violin musicals in the parlor and the study of classical thinkers such as Plato and Socrates. Nothing wrong with that at all.

But of course it was Septemus's aspersions on James's own character that really had the boy angry. Hinting that James was a pantywaist and a mother's boy; hinting that at this rate he'd never grow up to be a man.

He lay shirtless on his back, a black fly crawling around on his red freckled face. Maybe he should tell Septemus about the time he got drunk on beer that Fourth of July night when everybody thought he'd gone up to bed; or maybe he should tell him about how many times he'd loaded cornsilk into a pipe bowl and smoked till he'd turned green; or maybe he should tell him about the time, a spring moon making him slightly mad, he'd nearly kissed Marietta right on the lips. Boy, wouldn't these things surprise Uncle Septemus? Wouldn't he then look at James in a very different way?

A pantywaist; a mama's boy. Just wait till he saw Septemus.

The knock startled him. He turned his head to face the door so quickly that a line of warm pain shot up the side of his neck.

"That you, Uncle Septemus?" he called, uneasy about opening the door unless he knew who it was. His mother had given him explicit instructions about not putting himself in a position where he'd ever be alone with a stranger.

And then he heard Septemus inside his head: see how she's turning you into a sissy, son? Somebody knocks on your door and you won't even go open it. Now is that how a real man would act, son? Is it?

He fairly flung himself off the bed, making loose fists of his hands, striding to the door. To heck with what his mother said. He was sixteen; he was on his way to becoming a man. He would open the door and—

Halfway there, he realized he didn't have his shirt on. He was sure he shouldn't open the door half naked.

Feeling foolish and vulnerable, he dashed to the chair on the back of which was his shirt. He snapped it up and put it on and buttoned it. Then he went back to the door.

James had seen few men this tall. Even without a hat, the top of the man's head touched the top of the door frame. In addition to that, he was fleshy in a middle-aged sort of way, somewhat jowly and with a loose belly pinched tight by a huge silver buckle on which the initials DD had been sculpted. He wore a western-style white shirt, a brown leather vest, dark brown trousers, and Texas-toed black boots. He looked a little sweaty from the heat and a little sour around his large, wry mouth. James couldn't read his eyes at all.

His grin was somewhat surprising. "I take it you're not Septemus, son."

"No, sir," James said, then immediately recalled what his uncle had said about being too deferential. "I'm sure not." He tried to make the last sound hard-bitten, but his voice had soared too high for that. He'd just spotted the six-pointed star that the man wore tucked half under his vest.

"You'd be—"

"His nephew."

"I see." The man put out a huge hand. James slid his own into the other man's grasp. When they shook, James felt like a pump handle that somebody was jostling mercilessly. When he returned his hand to his side. James tried not to feel the pain the big man's hand had inflicted on him. "I'm Dodds."

"Dodds?"

"The sheriff."

"And you want to see my uncle Septemus?"

"If I could."

"He's not here."

The grin again. "I kinda figured that out for myself, son, I mean, I can see the whole room from here and I can see that it's empty except for you."

James flushed, knowing he'd been gently but absolutely shown his place.

"Any idea where I could find him?"

"Huh-uh."

"Any idea when he'll be back?"

"He said a couple of hours."

"How long ago was that?"

"'Bout an hour, I guess."

"Will you remember to tell him that Sheriff Dodds is lookin' for him?"

"Doesn't seem like the kind of thing I'd forget to mention."

This time the grin was accompanied by a whiskey laugh. "Say, you were bound and determined to pay me back for that crack I made, weren't you?"

James felt himself flush again. That's just what he'd been doing. Trying to show Dodds that he was a lot smarter than the lawman might think. "Guess so."

Dodds lifted the white Stetson he'd been keeping in his hand and cuffed James on the shoulder. "Damn straight, son. I've got a smart mouth on me and every once in a while somebody needs to put me in my place." He grinned again. "Damn straight."

Then he nodded and was gone.

James closed the door. He thought about lying down but he was too stirred up now. What would a sheriff want with Uncle Septemus?

He went over to the window and the billowing sheer curtain and stuck his head out. It was like leaning into an oven. Even though the water wagon had been over the dusty main street once today, dust devils rose in the still, chalky air. A crow sitting on the gable to James's right looked over at the boy with sleepy curiosity. The bird looked too tired to move.

There was no sign of Uncle Septemus.

James looked in every direction this particular window afforded. Then he looked again and saw nothing.

What the hell would a lawman want with his uncle?

He took his shirt off and went back and lay on the bed. There was no possibility of a nap now. He was too churned up.

Nor was he any longer angry with his uncle about the man implying he was a mama's boy. They could settle that particular matter later.

He lay on the bed. Another black fly started walking around on his red freckles.

What the hell would a lawman want with Uncle Septemus, anyway?

3

"You telling me you don't believe in a divine being?"

"No. I'm just telling you that I'm tired of a prayer that goes on for five minutes."

"It's not just another prayer, Dennis. It's grace. It's thanking the Lord for all his wonderful gifts."

"And just what gifts would those be?" Dennis Kittredge asked his wife.

They were at the dining room table, the festive one with the red and white oilcloth spread over it, a small blue blown-glass butter dish the shape of a diamond, and a pair of salt and pepper shakers got up to look like stalks of sweet corn.

His wife Mae was a small and fine-boned woman who was given to excessively high collars and excessively long skirts and excessively stern looks. In her youth she'd been high fine company, a tireless attender of county fairs and ice cream socials, and a somewhat daring lover. While they had never committed the ultimate sin in the time before their vows, they had many nights come very, very close: especially downriver near the dam where fireflies glowed like jewels against the ebony sky, and there was music to be heard in the silver water splashing down on the sharp rocks below.

Then two years after their marriage Mae had become pregnant, but she'd lost the child in a bloody puddle in the middle of the night, on a white sleeping sheet she'd later burned.

Ever since then she'd been lost to God. Her juices had seemed to dry up till she was an old and indifferent woman about sex, and even worse about festivities. Nights, after Kittredge was home from the farms where he worked for twenty-three cents an hour, she played the saw as her mother had taught her, and in the soft fitful glow of the kerosene lamp read him the Bible, the only part of which he cared anything for being the Book of Job. Oh, yes; Job was a man Kittredge could believe, all pain and rage and dashed expectations. The rest of the biblical prophets struck him as stupid and they bored him silly. But Job . . .

"You ready now?" she said, as if he were a little boy she had only to wait out.

He sighed, a scarecrow of a man with a long, angular face and furious black brows and dead cornflower blue eyes. "Yeah, I'm ready."

"Then proceed."

Why the hell did he stay here anymore? It was like living with your maiden aunt. But where else could he go?

He said grace and he said it the way he knew she wanted him to. No mumbling, no sloppy posture. He sat up bolt straight and he spoke in clear, loud words, with his head bowed: "Bless us O Lord for these our gifts . . ."

There was one sure way to irritate her; to keep your head up or spend your time eating up the food with your eyes.

"God likes it better when you bow your head," she'd told him once. So that was that. Ever since then he'd bowed his head. It just wasn't worth the grief he'd have gotten otherwise.

"You say it nice," she said when he'd finished and was already helping himself to the boiled potatoes and tomatoes and chicken. "You've got such a strong, manly voice and the Lord appreciates that."

He glanced up at her for a dangerous moment. He almost asked: And just how do you know all these things the Lord wants so much? Does he come and visit you at night after I'm asleep? Or maybe he comes during the day while I'm working; comes in and helps himself to the teakettle and sits in the wooden rocker next to the window and tells you exactly what he wants me and you to do. It must be something like that, Mae, because there's no other way you could possibly know so much about his likes and dislikes. No other possible way.

But he couldn't ever bring himself to do this because then he'd remember the horror he'd seen in her the night she'd miscarried on the bed in there, and the way her skinny white fingers had so reverently touched the bloody puddle, as if that itself were her child. Even after the doctor left she'd been unable to talk, and then he'd held her on his lap in the darkness in the rocker by the moonlit window. She'd surprised him by staying still, no tears and no words, just the rocker creaking until the crows and the roosters woke at dawn, and every once in a while he'd look at her face, at the worn-out girl of her and the birdy but pretty woman she'd become. And he'd realized then that he was holding a woman so sorrowful she was beyond any human solace, beyond it for the rest of their lives. Oh, in the spring they'd tried to have another child but it hadn't worked, nor had the attempt a year later. It was sometime then that she'd become so religious and it was around then that he'd lost his job over at Rochester and it was after that that the bank robbery went so wrong and the little girl was killed.

"Thank you," he said.

She looked up from cutting her chicken. "Thank you?"

"For saying that about my voice."

"Oh." She offered him one of her rare smiles, and he saw in the smile the girl she'd been, the girl he'd fallen in love with. "Well, you know it's true. All my friends used to say they wished their men had voices like yours."

He stopped eating. "Maybe it'd do you good to see them."

"Who?"

"Your old friends. Susan and Irma and Jane Marie."

She shrugged. "Oh, I see them every once in a while but I embarrass them." She shook her head. "They think I'm too religious. A fanatic." She looked straight at him and broke his heart with her madness. "They don't seem to know that the Lord is walking right alongside them and judging everything they do. Why, if we hadn't sinned before we were married, we'd probably have us three fine young children today."

This was another point in the conversation when he had to stop himself from speaking. Maybe it was the only way she could understand not being able to bear a child—through something she'd done wrong. But to him it was just sad foolishness, a judgment on them both, and just one more way in which he felt separated from her.

She patted his bony hand with her bony hand. It felt funny, like the cold touch of a stranger. "You're a good man, Dennis. The Lord's going to reward you on Judgment Day. You wait and see if he don't."

She had just settled into eating again, when they heard the neighbor dog yip and saw a shadow fall on the grass outside the kitchen window. Somebody was knocking on the back door.

"You finish eating," Kittredge said. "I'll get it."

He did not like who he saw framed in the door.

"Who is it?" Mae asked.

He decided to lie. Mae was harsh on the few friends he could claim. He'd convinced her he'd long ago given up the likes of Carlyle. "Kid from the smithy. I'll step outside. Want a smoke anyway."

She nodded to his plate. "You ain't finished yet, Dennis. You know how I worry about you."

And that was the terrible hell of it. She did love him and did worry about him just as he loved her and worried about her. But it was passionless. They might as well have been sister and brother.

He went outside into the fading day, into the fading heat of the fading day, and the first thing he did, right there on the stoop where his pa and grandpa had stood generations before him, was slap Carlyle right across the mouth.

"You know better than this," Kittredge said.

More humiliated than hurt, Carlyle touched the spot where the slap still burned and looked at Kittredge out of his poorshanty hurt and his poorshanty pain and said, "Onliest reason I did it was 'cause Griff told me to."

"Griff told you to come here?"

"That's exactly what he told me."

"I don't believe it."

"You go ask him."

"You know what my missus still thinks of the likes of you."

"Well, maybe I don't think a whole hell of a lot more of her, truth be told. You ever think of that? She gets flies on her shit the same way I do."

Kittredge looked back at the door, through the glass to where Mae had her head down eating. She never gained weight; there was a rawness to her skinniness. He looked back at Carlyle. "You don't use language like that in this house." Carlyle smirked. That was how Kittredge always thought of Carlyle—that poorshanty smirk over a dirty joke or a jibe that hurt somebody's feelings. "You know better than to push it with me, Carlyle. Least you should."

"Griff wants to see us. Tonight."

"Why?"

"West end of the Second Avenue bridge. Nine o'clock."

"You heard what I asked. Why?"

Carlyle shook his head. The smirk reappeared. He liked to smirk when he told you something that was going to scare you. He said, "That little girl's father came to town this afternoon."

"You're crazy, Carlyle. How could he track us down?"

"I don't know how he done it; but he done it. He's here and he's got a Winchester and he means to kill us." Carlyle ran a trembling hand over his sweaty head. "He was waitin' for me when I left Griff's."

"He tell you he means to kill us?"

"Pretty much."

"Pretty much doesn't mean that's what he's got in mind."

Carlyle shrugged. "You wasn't there. You didn't see his eyes, Kittredge."

"Your food's getting cold, dear," Mae called from the table.

Carlyle smirked. "Must be nice havin' a little lady call you 'dear' like that all the time."

"I'm not going to believe any of this till it's proven to me," Kittredge said.

"You better be there tonight or Griff's gonna be mad."

"I didn't know that Griff had become my boss."

"You better," Carlyle said, sounding like a little kid. "You better."

Then he turned and started away, into a path made golden by the fading rays of sunlight. When he was nothing more than a silhouette of flame, he turned back to Kittredge and said, "You shoulda seen his eyes, Kittredge. You shoulda seen 'em."

Then he was gone.

Chapter Three

1

When Uncle Septemus came back into the hotel room, he took off his hat, vest, and coat, set the Winchester against the bureau, and came over and lay down on the bed across from James.

James was reading a yellowback about cowboys and Indians. The hero was a man named Chesmore who, it seemed, changed disguises every few pages.

From his carpetbag on the floor next to the bed, Uncle Septemus took a pint bottle of rye, swigged some, then put his head down and closed his eyes. He left the bottle, corked, lying on his considerable belly.

"You trying to take a nap, Uncle Septemus?"

Uncle Septemus opened one brown eye and looked at James. "Guess I was till you asked me if I was."

"A man came."

"A man?"

"A lawman."

"A lawman?"

"The sheriff."

Uncle Septemus propped himself up uncomfortably, still giving James the benefit of only one eye. "He say what he wanted?"

"Said he wanted to talk to you."

"He say about what?"

James was careful not to say "No sir" and sound too deferential. "Nope."

Uncle Septemus closed his eye, lay back down flat, uncorked the rye bottle with his thick fingers, poured a considerable tote down his throat, corked up the bottle good, then gave the impression that he was deep asleep.

"Uncle Septemus?"

"Yes, son?"

"I know you're tryin' to sleep."

"If you know I'm tryin' to sleep, why are you bothering me then."

"Because, I guess."

"Because?"

"Aren't you worried?"

"About what?"

"About why a sheriff would come up to our room and ask to see you."

"Maybe he's somebody I know."

"Huh?"

"Maybe he's somebody who came to my store and bought things before. A lot of people do that, and from all over the area, because

I've got such good merchandise. They remember me but I don't remember them. Whenever I visit other towns, there's always somebody who comes running up and asks me do I remember him."

"You really think that's why the sheriff came up here?"

"Your mother sure has turned you into a worrier, hasn't she, James?"

There he went again. Another jibe at James's mother. "Uncle Septemus."

Septemus sighed. His eyes had remained closed and he was obviously getting irritated. "What is it now, James?"

"I don't want you to insult my mother anymore."

"I haven't insulted your mother. I've just expressed my concern that a woman can't turn a boy into a man. Only another man can do that. Nothing against your mother at all. She's a fine woman. a fine woman."

"You really mean that?"

"I really mean that."

Now James lay down and closed his eyes. The black fly was back, walking on his red freckles.

Uncle Septemus said, "I want you to wear that fancy linen collar tonight."

"Where are we going?"

"Someplace special." He hesitated. Now he rolled over and up onto one elbow. He looked at James with both eyes. "Look at me, James."

James rolled over on the bed across from his uncle and opened his eyes.

"Do you want me to be treated like a man?"

"Sure."

"A man can give his word to keep a secret and then keep that word. Do you think you can do that?"

"Does this have something to do with the sheriff?"

"Forget about the sheriff, James. This has nothing to do with him at all. This has to do with you being a man. Now can you give me your word that you can keep a secret?"

"Yes."

"Then I'll tell you that tonight I'm going to take you someplace very special."

"The opera house?"

"Nope."

"The racetrack?"

"Nope."

"The nickelodeon parlor?"

"Don't even try to guess. It's someplace so special you wouldn't guess it in a hundred years. Now let's take a nap."

So James lay back down. In the stillness of the dying afternoon, the stillness and dust and heat of the dying afternoon, he heard the clatter of horses and wagons and the shouts of men and the fading laughter of children. This town was very much like Council Bluffs and, thinking about home, James just naturally thought of Marietta.

But then he forgot Marietta because of his uncle's promise of something "special" this evening.

James wondered what it could possibly be.

2

People made jokes about the way Dodds kept his office. Three times a week he had it dusted, twice a week he had the floor mopped and waxed, and once a week he had the front windows cleaned. When his fancy rolltop desk was open visitors could see that his fastidiousness continued into his personal belongings as well. Everything had its proper drawer or slot. Nothing was left loose inside the desk except a small stack of almost blindingly white writing paper on which Dodds wrote in a labored but beautiful hand, always in ink with an Easterbrook steel pen. He had a son in Tucson and one in New York, and he wrote to them frequently. His wife dead, the sons were the only family he had left and corresponding was the only way he could stay in contact with them.

Unfortunately, they weren't so good about writing back. One of the sons had gone and had a baby, Dodds's first grandson, but before Dodds knew anything about the birth let alone the pregnancy, the kid, named Clarence, was born and already walking around his home in New York, where his father worked as an accountant. Dodds lived in a sleeping room two short blocks from the sheriff's office. He'd moved here after the missus died, selling the white gabled house they'd lived in on the edge of town, and making himself available to whatever kind of trouble arose.

Many nights you could see Dodds running down the middle of the street still pulling his suspenders up. The law—the jail, more exactly—was Dodds's life. He was sixty-one and would soon enough retire, and he meant to store up as many war stories as possible. He had some good ones. A drunken Indian, defiant beyond imagining because Dodds had arrested his brother, snuck into the office one night, jimmied up the rolltop desk and took a crap right in it. Then he'd locked the desk back up and waited for Dodds to come in and learn what had happened.

Another time Dodds had swum out against a hard current on a rainy day and rescued a two-month-old lamb that had fallen into the river. And then there was the Windsor woman, a genuine redheaded beauty with a touring opera company, a woman who also managed to steal a goodly number of diamonds and jewels and rubies from the local gentry who'd given her a fancy party. Oh, yes, he had some good tales, and he loved to tell them, too, over a bucket of beer on cool nights inside screened-in porches. It was too much trouble to find another woman and, anyway, he couldn't ever imagine loving anybody else the way he had Eva; so he said to hell with it and indulged himself in those pleasures that can only be enjoyed by solitary people. Such as being a fussbudget, which he most certainly was. It was said among the town's lawyers that you might not piss off Sheriff David Dodds by breaking into his room in the middle of the night but you'd piss him off for sure if you wore muddy boots while doing it.

Now Dodds sat at his desk, rolling his Easterbrook pen between his fingers the way he would a fine cigar, thinking about the former

Pinkerton man he'd run in last fall for being drunk and disorderly. O'Malley, the man's name had been. For the first week O'Malley had been there, Dodds hadn't been able to figure out what the man was doing in Myles. The check he'd run indicated that O'Malley had been let go from the Pinkertons. When that happened, it usually meant that the man had been found morally corrupt in some way; Alan Pinkerton was a stickler. So what was O'Malley doing there? During the long and noisy night that O'Malley had spent in one of the cells in back, he'd given Dodds at least some notion of why he'd come to Myles. A man had hired him to find out who had killed his daughter. Dodds had thought immediately of the killing in Council Bluffs, so it was not difficult to intuit from that that O'Malley was looking for those bank robbers people had been seeking so long.

During O'Malley's last three days in Myles, Dodds had followed him everywhere. He never learned exactly who O'Malley had decided on but, given the places he stopped at, O'Malley seemed to be giving most of his attention to three men—Griff, Kittredge, and Carlyle. Then O'Malley was gone.

Since then, Dodds had kept close watch on the three men, noting that while Griff and Kittredge saw each other occasionally, they stayed clear of Carlyle. The three men used to be close friends. He wondered what had gone wrong between them.

Earlier this afternoon, when he saw Septemus Ryan and James ride into town, he knew immediately that he was looking at the man who had hired the Pinkerton. He remembered from pictures that this was the man whose little girl had been killed.

He liked trouble, Dodds did. He believed it kept him young. He sensed that he was now going to have plenty of trouble, and very soon.

The black man and the Mexican in the next cell stared at the nineteen year old who was balled up on his straw cot like a sick colt.

"Couldn't you let me go till my pa gets here? You know he'll go my bail, Sheriff."

"I suppose he will. But that don't mean I can let you go. I didn't hand down that sentence. Judge Sullivan did. And there ain't a damn thing I can do about it, even if I wanted to."

"All I did was raise a little hell."

Dodds had been in the cell block with this kid for ten minutes now. It was enough. He didn't especially like seeing a boy like this thrown in with a bunch of hardcases, but then again, the kid should have thought about what he was doing when he got drunk the night before and shot up a tavern. He could have killed a few people in all that ruckus.

Dodds went to the cell door and called for his deputy to let him out. Dodds never took any chances. Only a fool brought keys into a cell with him.

Through the bars on the high windows, Dodds could see that it was getting dark. His stomach grumbled. He was looking forward to meat loaf and mashed potatoes and peas at Juanita's Diner down the street. It was Tuesday and that was the Tuesday menu.

Deputy Harrison, a twenty-five year old with lots of ambition and a certain cunning, but not much intelligence, came through the cell-block door and said, "The pretty boy here giving you any trouble, Sheriff? If he is, I'd be happy to take care of him for you."

"No, no trouble," Dodds said, weary of Harrison's bluff swaggering manner. Dodds had two deputies, Windom and Harrison. Widom possessed wisdom but no courage and Harrison possessed courage but no wisdom. Together they made Dodds one hell of a deputy.

"Had to come back and get you anyway, Sheriff," Harrison said.

"Oh?"

"Yep. You got a visitor."

"Visitor? Who?"

"Man named Ryan. Septemus Ryan."

"Here you were looking for me, Sheriff."

Up close, Ryan gave the same impression he had riding into town this afternoon. A kind of arrogance crossed with a curious sadness.

The mouth, for instance, was wide and confident, even petulant; but the brown eyes were aggrieved, and deeply so.

Ryan put out a hand. He had one damn fine grip.

"Coffee, Mr. Ryan?"

"Sounds good."

When they were seated on their respective sides of Dodds's desk, tin cups of coffee hot in their hands, Dodds said, "You look familiar to me, Mr. Ryan."

Ryan smiled. "You were probably a customer of mine at one time or another. Ryan's Male Attire in Council Bluffs. The finest fabrics and appointments outside Chicago." He smiled again. He had a nice, ingratiating smile. His brown eyes were as sad as ever. "If I do say so myself."

Dodds decided not to waste any time. "I saw your picture in the state newspaper not too long ago."

Ryan just stared at him with those handsome brown eyes.

"They was lowering a casket into a grave and you was standing topside of that grave. They was burying your daughter, Mr. Ryan. Or are you going to deny that that was you?"

Ryan shook his head.

Dodds leaned forward on his elbows. "Then not too long ago an ex-Pinkerton man came to Myles. He seemed to be looking for somebody special." A hard smile broke Dodds's face. "He probably didn't tell you this part, Mr. Ryan, but one night he got drunk and in a fight down the street, and I had to bring him back here to cool him off for the night, and during that night he told me all about this man who'd hired him. I got a good notion of who that man would be, Mr. Ryan."

Ryan continued to stare at him. There was no reading those eyes, no reading them at all.

"You were the one who hired him. And I know why, too. You had him backtrackin' the men who killed your girl. And that eventually led him here. Isn't that about right, Mr. Ryan?"

"I'd be a foolish man to interrupt a sheriff as well-spoken as you."

"So now you're here, Mr. Ryan, and there can only be one reason for that."

"And what would that be, Sheriff?"

"You plan to take the law into your own hands. You plan to kill those three men."

Ryan sat back in his chair. "Are you going to arrest me, Sheriff?"

"Wish I could. All I can do right now is warn you. I'm not a man who abides vengeance outside the law. I grew up near the border, Mr. Ryan, and I got enough lynch-law justice in my first fifteen years to last me a lifetime. I seen my own brother hanged by a pack of men, and I seen an uncle of mine, too. It's one thing I don't tolerate."

Ryan kept his eyes level on Dodds's. "Oh, I expect there's a lot you don't tolerate, Sheriff Dodds."

"And why the hell'd you bring that boy along? If I ever seen a sweeter young kid, I don't know when or where it'd be."

"Maybe that's his problem. Maybe he's too sweet for his own good."

"So you invite him along so he can see you kill three men?"

"You're the one who keeps saying that, Sheriff, about me killing those three men. Not me."

Dodds's chair squawked as he leaned back. "I make a bad enemy, Mr. Ryan. I'm warning you now so you won't make no mistakes about it. When I took this job twenty years ago, it wasn't safe to walk the streets. My pride is that I made it safe and I mean to keep it safe."

Ryan drained his coffee and set the cup down on the edge of the desk. "That about the extent of what you've got to say?"

"That would be about it, Mr. Ryan."

"Then I guess I'll get back to my nephew. Promised him a fancy dinner and a good time in your little town."

Dodds pawed a big hand over his angular face. "If you've got proof they're really the killers, Mr. Ryan, give me the proof and let me take them in. I'd be glad to help hang the men who murdered your daughter."

Ryan stood up. "I appreciate the offer, Sheriff. And I'll definitely think it over."

With that, he tilted his derby at a smart-aleck angle, nodded goodbye to Dodds, and went out the front door.

Dodds listened to the front door close, the little bell above the frame tinkling. He sat there for a time thinking about Ryan and his brown eyes and what those brown eyes said. Sorrow, to be sure; and then Dodds realized what else—it could be heard in his laugh and seen in his smile, too—craziness, pure blessed craziness, the kind you'd feel if somebody killed your little girl and got away with it.

3

It was a place of Rochester lamps whose light was the color of burnished gold; of starchy white tablecloths; of waiters in walrus mustaches and ladies in low-cut organdy gowns. Several tables away from where James sat with him Uncle Septemus, a pair of men got up to resemble gypsies walked around the restaurant, dramatically playing their violins. Even though nobody paid much attention—and even though some of the men looked damned uncomfortable with such displays of passion and emotion—the would-be gypsies lent the place its final touch of sophistication.

"They kind of make me nervous," James confided.

"Who?"

"Those gypsies."

"Why should they make you nervous?"

"I don't know. Like they'd just sneak up behind you all of a sudden."

"And then what?"

"I don't know. Play some really corny song."

"And embarrass you?"

James nodded. "Yeah, sort of."

Uncle Septemus raised his wineglass. He was notorious,

within the family, for being an easy drunk. He'd had three glasses of wine so far this evening, and he was showing the effects. His words slurred, and his handsome brown eyes seemed not quite focused.

"Wait till you're a little older," Septemus said.

"Then what?"

Septemus smiled. "Then you'll appreciate things more."

"Like gypsy violinists?"

Septemus laughed. "Like gypsy violinists." And then his smile died. "And memories."

The silver tears came clear and obvious in his brown eyes. "Do you ever think about her, James?"

"Who?"

"Why, Clarice, of course. My daughter."

James felt embarrassed. He should have known who his uncle was talking about. Much of the time, his uncle talked about little else. "Sure."

"Are you just saying that?"

"Huh-uh, Uncle Septemus, honest."

Septemus drank from his goblet and then rolled the wine around the fine glass that filled his hand. Septemus was a lover of fine foods, he was. "What's your favorite memory of her?"

"My favorite?" James was stalling for time. His favorite? He'd never thought of it that way. "Uh . . ."

"Don't worry," Septemus said. "I have the same problem. I have so many good memories, I don't know which one is my favorite."

"When we used to go sledding, is one of them. She never got afraid like the other girls. She'd come lickety-split down those hills and sail right onto Hartson Creek. Not afraid at all."

Septemus smiled again, looking beyond James now. James wondered what he was seeing.

Septemus said, "Winter was her favorite time. You'd think it would've been spring or summer or even fall but no, it was winter. I remember how she used to get snow all over her face so it looked like she had these big bushy white eyebrows and how red her cheeks would get and how her eyes would sparkle. I think about her eyes a lot."

James was afraid his uncle was going to start sobbing right in the middle of the restaurant. James was never prepared for such scenes. All he could do was kind of sit there and sort of scooch down in his seat and more or less hold his breath and hope for the best.

Septemus said, leaning across, "If I tell you something, will you promise not to tell your mother?"

"Uh-huh."

"You promise?"

"Honest, Uncle Septemus. Honest."

"Because she worries about me. I'm sure she's told you I'm not quite right in the head since Clarice was killed."

James felt his cheeks get hot. That's exactly what his mother had told him, and many times.

"No, Uncle Septemus, she never said anything like that."

"She talks to me. All the time." Uncle Septemus was staring right at James now.

"My mother?"

"No, Clarice."

"Clarice talks to you?"

"Clear as bell. Usually at night, just when I'm going to sleep."

"Oh."

Septemus's eyes seemed to press James back in his chair. "You don't believe me, do you, James?"

"No, I believe you."

"Do you think I'm crazy?"

"No, Uncle Septemus, I don't." He hesitated before speaking again. "I just think you miss her an awful lot."

"More than you can imagine, James."

"It was like when Blackie died."

"Your dog?"

"Uh-huh. He was all I thought about all last summer. Sometimes I'd look up on the hill by the railroad tracks and I'd see him running there, black as all get out and going lickety-split, but when I'd tell Mom about it, she'd just kind of get sad looking and say, 'You'll get over it, dear.' But I saw Blackie; I'm sure I did. And I'm sure Clarice speaks to you, too. I'm sure of it, Uncle Septemus."

The tears were back. "You're a good boy, James, and I love you very much. I want you to know that."

"I do know that, truly."

"And those things I said about being brought up by a man—I only meant it for your own good."

"I know."

"The world's a harsh enough place but for men who can't deal with it—it's especially harsh for men like that, if you know what I'm talking about."

"I know. My friend Ronnie's got a cousin like that. People make fun of him all the time and about all he can do is run away and hide. It must be awful."

"You can bet it is awful, James." He sipped some more wine. "I'll say hello for you next time."

"To Clarice?"

"Umm-hmm. If you'd like me to."

"Tell her I'm thinking about her."

Septemus smiled again. "I'll be happy to tell her that, James. Happy to."

Septemus raised his wineglass. "But for now, let's toast our adventure for tonight."

"Our adventure? Is that the surprise you were telling me about?"

"Indeed it is, James. Indeed it is." Earlier Septemus had asked the waiter for two wineglasses. One had stood empty for the length of the dinner. Now Septemus filled it halfway up and handed it over to James.

"Maybe I hadn't ought to," James said. "You know how my mother is with us kids. She won't even let us sample the cider."

"You're with me now, James, not with your mother."

"You sure it's all right?"

"It's man to man tonight, James. It's what's expected of you."

Septemus raised his glass in toast again. "Now raise yours, James."

James raised his.

"Now we'll toast," Septemus said, and brought his glass against James's. "To our adventure tonight. Now you say it, James."

"To our adventure tonight."

"Perfect." They clinked glasses.

"Uncle Septemus," James said after he'd had a sip of wine and the stuff tasted sweet and hot at the same time in his throat.

"Yes?"

"What exactly is our adventure going to be, anyway?"

"You mean you haven't figured it out yet?"

"Huh-uh."

"You really haven't?"

"Honest, Uncle Septemus. I can't figure it out at all."

"Well, tonight's the night you become a man."

"I do?"

"You do." Septemus looked across the table with great patriarchal pride. He smiled. "Tonight I'm taking you to a whorehouse."

Chapter Four

1

"You going out?"

"Thought I might take a walk," Dennis Kittredge said.

"You be gone long?"

"Not too long."

"You thinking of stopping by the tavern?"

He was by the front door, the lace covering the glass smelling of dry summer dust. In the trees near the curb he could see the dying day, flame and dusk and a half moon. "I might have me a glass or two is all."

She was in the rocker, knitting, a magazine in her lap. He'd seen the magazine earlier. It had a painting of a very pretty Jesus on it. Jesus was touching his glowing heart with long fingers. "You forgetting what night it is?"

"I'm not fogetting."

"I don't often ask that you pray with me but I don't see how fifteen minutes one night a week is going to help."

"And just what is it we're praying for?"

She paused and looked down at her poor worn hands. She worked so hard and sometimes he felt terrible for resenting her prayerfulness. She looked up then. "I had the dream again last night."

"I see."

"Don't you want to know which one?"

"I know which one."

"The son we would've had. I saw him plain on a hill right at dawn. He was running right toward us. We were on a buckboard on a dusty road and we didn't hear him or see him. He kept running and running and shouting and shouting but we didn't see him or hear him. Finally, he fell down in the long grass and all the animals came to him at night and comforted him—because we wouldn't comfort him."

Kittredge sighed. "I won't be gone too long."

"Don't you know what the dream could mean?"

"No. I guess I don't."

"Why, it could mean that He's forgiven us, that the Lord has forgiven us for sinning before we were married, and that now He's ready to let us have children."

"I see."

"Don't you believe that, Dennis?"

"I'm not sure just what I do believe," he said, and pulled the door open. The sounds and smells of dusk—the robins and jays in the trees, a hard relentless chorus, the scent of flowers as they cooled in the dusk—he took all this in with great affection. He wanted to be out in the night, a part of all this.

"I won't be gone too long," he said again, and before she could respond he was out the door and moving fast toward the sidewalk.

He liked walking downtown at night. He liked the way the lamplight glowed and the way women in picture hats and bustles walked on the arms of their gentlemen to the opera house where shiny coaches and rigs stood outside waiting. He liked the sound of player pianos on the lonely midwestern darkness and he liked the smell of brewer's yeast that you picked up as you passed tavern doors. He liked the sound of pinochle and poker hands being slapped down on the table, and the sweet high giggle of tavern maids. This was, by God, 1901 and this was, by God, civilized and he took a curious pride in this, as if he were personally responsible for it all.

It was not quite eight o'clock, so he walked down to the roundhouse tavern where the railroad men drank. It was his favorite place unless there were too many Mexicans in there from some road crew. He hated the way Mexicans resorted to their knives so quickly; he'd seen it too many times. A man stabbed was much worse than a man shot—at least to the man watching it all.

The place was nearly empty. At the far end of the plank bar two Mexes drank from a bucket of suds, and at the other a white man played blackjack with the bartender. In the corner a player piano rolled out the melody to "My Sweet Brown Eyes" while an old man, nodding off in his cups, lay facedown on the pianos keys, spittle running silver from his mouth to the floor. The bartender paid him no mind.

A maid appeared from the back and served Kittredge his beer. He stood there with his schooner, enjoying the player piano. It was playing Stephen Foster songs now, a medley, and his toe tapped and in just a few swallows he felt buzzy, not drunk, but buzzy and blessedly so. He forgot that in an hour he would meet Griff and Carlyle and that together they would have to decide what to do about Septemus Ryan. That was the funny thing about the whole event: he did not feel responsible. It had been an accident, though obviously most people had chosen not to believe that, an accident because Dennis Kittredge was a good and responsible man and had been all his life.

He felt that if he could open his heart and look inside he would find fine things—patience and courage and understanding. He was not the sort of man who cut up other men the way Mexes did and he was certainly not the sort of man who killed young girls. It all had a dreamy quality to it. He would always be, in his heart, the little kid making his first communion—why couldn't people understand that?

"Nice night for a walk."

Kittredge turned around and saw Sheriff Dodds standing there. The sheriff tossed a nickel on the bar plank. The maid brought him a schooner with a good foamy head on it.

"Sure is," Kittredge said.

The sheriff sipped his beer, studying Kittredge as he did so. "You still think about the days when the wagon works was up and runnin'?"

"Sure. Everybody does."

"Them was good times."

"Sure was."

"Hell," Dodds said, "I remember seein' you and Griff and Carlyle everywhere I went. You three was some friends."

"Some friends is right," Kittredge said, then swigged some of his own beer. For some reason, his stomach was knotting and he had started having some problems swallowing, the way he did sometimes when he got nervous. Dodds came in there often enough, had a schooner or two a night, nothing to scandalize even church ladies, and often as not he spoke to Dennis, too. But there was something about his tone tonight, as if he were saying one thing but meaning quite another. Kittredge wondered what the hell Dodds was driving at.

"You boys don't hang around each other much anymore, do you?"

"Guess we don't, Sheriff."

"Too bad. You bein' such good friends and all. At one time, I mean." He said this over the rim of his schooner. He was still watching Kittredge very closely.

Kittredge looked toward the door. "Well," he said.

Dodds followed his gaze to the front of the tavern. "Going on home now?"

Kittredge met his glance. "Thought I might finish my walk."

"I'd be careful if I were you."

"Careful?"

Dodds drained off his beer. "Hear there are some strangers in town."

"Why would strangers bother me?"

"Well, you know how it is with strangers. You can never be sure what they want."

Now Kittredge finished his own beer. He belched a little because he'd put it down too fast. "Well, guess I'll be saying goodnight, Sheriff."

But Dodds wasn't done. Not quite. "Too bad you don't have any children, Kittredge."

"Yep. I suppose it is." What the hell was Dodds getting at, anyway?

"Man who don't have no children of his own don't know what it means to lose one. Take this man a while back, this Ryan fella, over in Council Bluffs. His little girl got killed in the course of a bank robbery."

"I guess I heard about that. Don't remember it all, quite."

"Little girl's father went insane, some people said. Just couldn't get over it. Hired an investigator fella to start backtrackin' the robbers. Guess the investigator fella had some good luck."

Kittredge felt faint. Actually, literally faint, the way women got. He put a hand for steadiness on the plank bar. "Sure hope they catch those thieves."

And all the while, remorseless, Dodds staring at him. Staring.

"If I was them boys, I'd be a lot more scared of Septemus Ryan than the law."

"Oh?"

"Law'll give them boys a fair hearing. If it was an accident that the little girl got killed, which some of the witnesses say it was, law'll take that into account."

"But not the little girl's father?"

"Oh, not the little girl's father at all. Put yourself in his place, Kittredge. Say you had a pretty little girl and one day she got killed like that. Wouldn't make no difference to you if it was an accident or not. Least it wouldn't to most fathers. All they'd want to do is kill the men who killed their pretty little girl. You ever think of it that way?"

"Ain't thought about it much one way or the other, Sheriff," Kittredge said. His voice was so dry he could barely speak, but he didn't want to order another schooner because then he'd have to stand there and drink it with Dodds.

Dodds nodded. "Well, if you ever do sit down and start thinking it over, Kittredge, that's just how I'd figure it—that I'd have me a much better chance with the lawn'n I would a grief-crazy father. You might pass that along to Griff and Carlyle, too?"

"Now why would they care about that, Sheriff?"

Dodds made a face. "Carlyle, he's too dumb and too shiftless to care. But Griff, well, he's smart. You tell him what I told you and he's likely to agree with me."

So he knew, Dodds did. There could be no mistaking. Somehow he'd found out about the robbery and the little girl and knew that it was the three of them who were involved.

Dodds said, "You have yourself a nice walk, Kittredge."

"I will."

"And you say hello to Mae. She's a fine woman; but I guess you know that."

"She is a fine woman, Sheriff, and I appreciate you sayin' that."

Imagine what Mae would think of him if she ever found out he was involved in the robbery of that bank and the death of that little girl.

"So long, Kittredge," Dodds said, then swung back so that he was facing the tavern maid. He ordered himself another schooner.

Kittredge left.

2

When James was younger, just after his father's funeral, his mother's sister, a shy and unmarried woman named Nella, stayed with the family for three months till, as she put it, Mrs. Hogan "saw that there were things still worth living for." It was Nella's habit to bathe in the downstairs bathroom, where the tub with the claws and the wall with the nymphs on it sat in the rear of the house. Nella always waited till everyone had gone to sleep before bathing. The family was too polite to ask why, of course, respecting their aunt as they did, even if she was "eccentric" as their mother had rather shamefully said of her one day.

One night, when he badly needed a drink, and had found his mother in the upstairs bathroom, James had gone downstairs, thinking he'd get water from the kitchen, which the colored maid had cleaned only that afternoon. He descended the stairs in darkness, liking the way winter moonlight played silver and frosty through the front window. Then he heard the sighing from the back of the house, from the bathroom.

At first the sound reminded him of pain. But why would Nella inflict pain on herself?

On tiptoe, sensing he should not do what he was about to do, James went down the hall to the bathroom. The closer he got the more pronounced the moaning and the signing became.

He was about to raise his hand and let it gently fall against the door when she said, "Oh, Donald; Donald." And that stopped him. Was there a man in there with her?

He did not knock. Instead he did what so many comedians in

vaudeville did. He fell to one knee and peered through the key hole.

Aunt Nella was nude. The body she had kept modestly hidden was beautiful and womanly and overwhelming to him. She leaned against the wall with the nymphs so that he could see her clearly, her eyes closed so tightly, her mouth open and gasping, her hand fallen and moving quicksilver fast at the part in her white legs. "Oh, Donald; Donald." And he saw now that she was alone and only summoning the man as if he were a ghost who could pass through walls and visit her, touch her as she now touched herself.

He never forgot how Aunt Nella looked that night; she would forever be the woman with whom he compared all other women, and for many years after, in stern midwestern February and in soft midwestern October, he would see her there projected on his ceiling. Oh, Nella; Nella (just as she'd called out for Donald). Nella.

Just after his third drink, just after Uncle Septemus disappeared down the hall, just after the door closed and the girl came in and dropped her shabby dress to her wide hips, James thought of Nella, thinking the most forbidden thought of all, that he wished it were Nella he was with on this most important of nights, and not some chubby farm girl with bleached hair and the smell of too-sweet perfume.

The whorehouse shook with the relentless happiness of player pianos (one up, one down) and the even more relentless happiness of girls determined in their somewhat sad way to show the men a good time. He could smell whiskey and cigar smoke and sweat, and could see the flickering shadows cast by the kerosene lamp on the sentimental painting of the innocent but somehow erotic young prairie girl above the brass bed. James supposed that that was how all the girls saw themselves—idealized and vulnerable in that way, not crude and harsh and defeated as they really were.

She came over and stood by him and said, "My name's Liz."

"Hi, Liz."

She smiled. "It's all right if you look at them. That's why I took my dress down. So you could see them."

He couldn't stop staring at her breasts. He'd raise his eyes and look into her eyes or he'd glance up at the painting above the bed but always his eyes would drop back down to her breasts.

She reached out and took his hand. Touched it in such a way that he could tell she was making some character judgment about him. "You're not a farm boy, are you?"

"No, ma'm."

She giggled. "I ain't no 'ma'm,' I bet I'm younger than you. I'm fourteen."

He didn't say anything. Stood straight and still, heart hammering.

"You want to kiss first?"

"I guess so," he said.

"You don't know what to do, do you?"

"I guess not."

"You look mighty scared."

He said nothing.

"If you just relax, you'll enjoy yourself."

He said nothing.

"You kinda remind me of my brother and that's kinda sweet." She leaned forward and kissed him gently on the lips. "That feel good?"

"I guess so."

She laughed. "You sure 'guess' about a lot of things."

He said nothing.

She took his hand again. She led him over to the bed. They sat on the edge of it, the springs squeaking. She was prettier in profile than straight on. He wanted her to be pretty. On a night like this you wanted your girl to be pretty. He wondered if he'd be so scared now if he were sitting here with Marietta. Or Nella. That was a terrible thought and he tried not to think it, about sitting there with his own aunt, but he couldn't help it.

He said, "Do you go to school?"

She turned and looked at him. "Do I go to school?" She smiled and patted his hand. "Honey, they wouldn't let girls like me in school."

"You got folks?"

"In South Dakota."

"Do they—"

"Do they know what I do? Was that what you were gonna ask me?"

"I guess."

"No. They don't know. A year ago I run off. This was as far as I got. I wrote 'em and tole 'em I'm working for this nice woman." She laughed. "Miss Susan is nice; that part of it ain't a lie."

He sat on the edge of the bed and stared down at his hands. They were trembling. "We don't have to do anything. I wouldn't ask for my money back, I mean."

"You afraid you can't do it?"

He didn't say anything.

"A lot of men are like that. Even when they've been doin' it regular all their lives. They just get kinda scared and they get worried if they're gonna make fools of themselves but, heck, you'll be fine."

"You sure?"

"Sure. I mean, we'll take it real slow. We'll lay back on the bed and just kind of hold each other and take it real slow. I like it better that way anyway."

"You do?"

"Sure. More like we care about each other."

"You want to lie back now?"

"You talk good, don't you?"

"Good?"

"Proper-like."

"English is one of my best subjects."

"She laughed. "Honey, none of 'em was my best subject. I'm thick as a log."

"You ready?"

"Any time you are."

"And I just lie back?"

"You just lie back."

"I don't take my clothes off yet?"

"Not yet. I'll do that for you later."

"And then we just . . . do it?"

"That's right. Then we just . . . do it. But maybe I should teach you a little trick."

"A trick?"

"I ain't a beautiful girl, honey. I know that. I got a nice set of milk jugs but that's about it. So Miss Sue tole me about this little trick to pass on to men."

"What sort of trick?"

She giggled. "You're getting scared again, honey. It's nothing to be scared about at all." She leaned over and touched his chest. He liked the weight and warmth of her pressed against him. "You got a sweetheart?"

James thought about it. Should he even mention Marietta's name to a girl like this? "I guess."

"Well, then, while we're doin' it, you close your eyes and pretend I'm her. It'll be a lot better for you that way."

"But isn't that kind of—" He shook his head.

"Kind of what?"

"Won't that kind of hurt your feelings?"

She looked up at him in the soft flicking lampglow. How hard she seemed, and yet there was a weariness in her young gaze that made him sad for her. She was fourteen and no fourteen year old he knew looked this weary. "Nope," she said. "It won't hurt my feelings at all."

But for some reason he didn't think she was telling him the truth. For some reason he thought she might be happy to hear what he said next.

"I'm happy to be with you," he said.

"You are?"

"Sure."

"Well, that's nice of you to say." She pointed to her mouth. "Let me finish chewin' my gum so my breath gets good and sweet."

She finished chewing her gum, then set it with surprising delicacy on the edge of the bureau and lay back down next to him.

"Would you like it better if I turned the lamp out?" she said.

"Yeah, maybe that would be better."

So she turned the lamp out.

He lay there in the darkness listening to both of them breathe.

After a time she kissed him and it was awkward and he felt nervous and afraid but then she kissed him a second and a third time and it felt very nice and he began stroking her bleached hair and she took one of his hands and set it to her breast and then everything was fine, just fine, and all the whorehouse noise faded and it was just them in the soft shared prairie shadows.

3

Tess was his littlest girl. She was four. Because of the heat she wore a pair of ribbed summer drawers. Her sister Eloise was asleep. Tess was at the doorway, giving Griff a hug he had to bend down to get. Her body was hot and damp and as always she felt almost frighteningly fragile in his arms. He kissed her blue eyes and her pink lips and then he hugged her, feeling the doll cradled in her arm press against him.

"Will you kiss Betty, too?"

"Kind of hot for a kiss, isn't it?" Griff said playfully.

"You kissed me, Daddy. Can't you kiss her?"

Griff looked over at his wife in the rattan rocker and winked. "Oh, I guess I could."

So he picked Betty up and kissed her on the forehead and handed her back.

"'Night, punkin'," he said, bending down and holding Tess to his leg. She was so small, she scarcely touched his thigh.

"Will you bring me ice cream?"

"I'm afraid I can't tonight, hon."

"How come?"

"I have some business to take care of."

"What kind of business?"

He laughed. "Dora, don't you think it's time you put your little girl to bed?"

Dora got up from the rocker and came over. She leaned down and picked up Tess. Tess held tight to Betty.

Dora said, "How about a kiss for me, too?"

Griff obliged. He held her longer than he meant to and he closed his eyes as he kissed her. He knew that she knew something was wrong. He'd told her that Kittredge wanted to talk to him about some haying later on in the fall, that the hay man wanted an answer tomorrow morning. But she knew. All during dinner he'd felt her eyes on him. Gray, loving, gentle eyes. Now, holding their youngest, she touched him and the feel of her fingers on his forearm made him feel weak, as if he were caught up in some kind of reverie. He wanted to be younger, back before the holdup and the little girl getting killed. How stupid it all seemed now, being so concerned about not having a job, feeling so afraid that he'd been pushed to such extremes. Hell, he didn't have nearly as good a job even now but they were making it and making it fine.

"You don't have to go, you know," Dora said. A tall woman, not pretty but handsome in her clean purposeful way, she tugged on his shirtsleeve much as Tess had done earlier. "You could always tell Kittredge you just weren't interested."

"Could be some good money. You never can tell."

She said, "Is Carlyle going to be there?"

"Carlyle? Why would he be there? I haven't seen Carlyle in a long time."

"It just feels funny, tonight."

"What's 'feel funny,' Momma?" Tess said.

He leaned in and kissed them both again. "I won't be too long," he said, and then he was gone.

Long before there was a brick-and-steel bridge near the dam, Griff used to go there as a boy and throw his fishing line in and spend the day. He'd always bring an apple, a piece of jerky, and enough water to last the long hot day. Other boys would come but

Griff always managed to stay alone, liking it better that way. But much as he liked it during the day, he liked it even better at night, when the water over the dam fell silver in the moonlight, and when fishermen in boats downriver could be seen standing up against the golden circle of the moon, casting out their lines and waiting, waiting for their smallmouth bass and catfish and sheepshead and northern pike. In the war, where he'd served in the Eleventh Infantry under General Ord during the siege of Corinth and the occupation of Bolivar, he'd lain awake nights thinking of his fishing spot, and the firefly darkness, and the rush and roar of the dam, and rainclouds passing the moon.

He was hoping to be a little early tonight so he could appreciate all this before Kittredge and Carlyle got there, but as soon as he left the main path over by the swings he saw two figures outlined against the sky and he knew that tonight there wouldn't be even that much peace.

Kittredge said, "Good thing you got here now. Carlyle's gone crazy."

"Crazy, hell," Carlyle said. "I'm just sayin' we should take care of him before he takes care of us."

Griff sighed. Things hadn't changed any in the years the men had been apart. Kittredge and Carlyle had never gotten along; it had always been up to Griff to keep things smooth between them. Tonight was especially bad. Even from several feet away, Griff could see and smell that Carlyle was drunk.

"Plus we've got some complications," Kittredge said. "And I don't mean just the little girl's father."

"What're you talking about?"

So Kittredge explained how Sheriff Dodds had come into the roundhouse tavern and pretty much said that he knew the three men had stuck up the bank and killed the little girl—maybe not killed her on purpose but killed her nonetheless—and that if he, Dodds, had to choose fates, he'd take his chances with the law instead of with some crazy man with a Winchester.

"That's why I say we kill Ryan," Carlyle said, "before he kills us."

"Shut up," Griff said.

They stood downslope from the dam so they cold talk over the roar. Griff rolled himself a cigarette, taking the smoke deep into his lungs, savoring the burning. He said, "Maybe we should take it to a vote."

"Take what to a vote?" Carlyle said.

"What the sheriff said."

"You mean turning ourselves in?" Kittredge said.

"Yup," Griff said. "Maybe that's the easiest way to do things."

"That what you want to do, Griff?" Carlyle said.

"I didn't say one way or the other; all I said was that maybe we should take it to a vote."

"I been in Fort Madison," Carlyle said. "I'd never last in there again. I'm too god damn old for prison."

"So you're voting against it?" Griff said.

"God damn right I'm votin' against it."

"Kittredge? What do you think we should do?"

Kittredge ran a hand across his face, turned slightly to look out at the water over the grassy hump of the slope, then spat into the earth. He turned back to his partners. "You think he'd listen to our side of it?"

"Who?" Griff said.

"Ryan."

"Doubt it," Griff said. "Put yourself in his place. Your daughter gets killed by three men and they come and try and tell you their side. Would you listen to them?"

Kittredge thought a moment. Then, "Maybe there's a third way, instead of turnin' ourselves in or just waitin' for Ryan to shoot us."

"What would that be?" Griff said.

"What Carlyle said."

"Damn right," Carlyle said. "What I said."

"Shoot Ryan, you mean?" Griff said.

"Yes."

"Damn right," Carlyle said again. "Let's vote right now."

Griff paid him no attention. He turned to Kittredge. "That's the tempting way, I know. But think about it. You said the sheriff pretty much believes we're the men involved in the robbery. But maybe he doesn't have hard evidence."

"So what?" Carlyle said.

Griff kept talking straight to Kittredge, even though Kittredge wasn't responding. "So if Ryan gets killed, who do you think the sheriff's going to blame? Us." He paused. "There's at least some possibility that the sheriff will never be able to prove we had a part in that robbery. But if we go after Ryan ourselves—"

"I want a damn vote," Carlyle said.

"He's right, Carlyle," Kittredge said.

"What?" Carlyle said.

"He's right. Griff is. By goin' after Ryan, we'd just be admitting that we were guilty."

"You votin' with him, then?"

"Yes," Kittredge said. "I am."

Griff allowed himself a small sigh. "We wait."

"We what?"

"We wait, Carlyle. We see what Ryan's going to do next. That's the only way we stay out of trouble."

"What if he tries to kill us?" Carlyle said.

"Then we have the sheriff take care of him. You know how Dodds is. He won't allow anybody to start shooting people. He'll either run Ryan in or run him out of town. Either way, he takes care of our problem for us."

"You make it sound pretty god damn simple," Carlyle said.

"It's a lot simpler than shooting somebody," Griff said, anger in his voice now. "You seem to forget something, Carlyle. We're not killers. Hell, we're not even thieves. We didn't get any money at all from that robbery. We killed a little girl by accident and we're going to fry in hell for what we did. But that still don't make us killers. That still don't mean we could pick up a gun and kill a man in cold blood." He nodded to Kittredge. "At least Kittredge and I couldn't." He turned back to Carlyle. "And I don't think you could, either. Not when you came right down to it. You like your hootch and you like your whores but that's a long damn way from bein' a killer."

"You didn't see his eyes this afternoon," Carlyle said.

"We killed his little girl. How do you think he'd look?" Griff said.

"So we wait?" Kittredge said.

"Yes," Griff said, "we just wait and see what happens."

"Shit," Carlyle said, and pulled away from the two men, wobbling drunkenly over to a huge elm tree. In the darkness they could hear him splashing piss against the tree.

"He's gets crazier the older he gets," Kittredge said.

Griff nodded. "The way I see it, we've got two problems."

"Two?"

"Ryan and Carlyle. Either one of them could do something crazy. Damn crazy."

Kittredge sighed. "My stomach's in knots. I couldn't eat tonight."

"We'll keep an eye on him," Griff said, "and we'll be alright."

But he couldn't muster much conviction in his voice. All he could do was just stand there and watch Carlyle come wobbling back, zipping up his pants as he moved through the grass.

Griff just wanted to be home in bed with his wife and have his daughters come laughing in just after dawn, ready for a new day. But he had the terrible feeling that that simple pleasure was beyond him now. Maybe forever.

"I still want a god damn vote on the subject," Carlyle said as he swerved up to the two men.

Which was when Griff slapped him hard across the mouth. Slapped him as hard as he could, hard enough to knock him to his knees.

"Maybe you shouldn't have done that," Kittredge said, sounding tense.

Griff nodded. "Maybe I shouldn't have."

"You sonofabitch, you sonofabitch," Carlyle said, furious but drunk enough that he could not get easily to his feet. "You sonofabitch."

Griff walked away from the other two men. He went over and stood by the dam, the silver foaming water falling in the mosquito-thick night air. Thirty years ago, the boy he'd been had stood here all filled with great unbounded hope. How could he have known that all these long years later he would be standing here, the killer of a little girl, and the little girl's father come to pay him back?

He shook his head and stared with great sorrow at the roaring, tumbling water.

Then he went back to tell Carlyle he was sorry for slapping him.

4

James did the most unlikely thing of all, fell asleep just after he finished making love to the girl. Several glasses of wine had made him drowsy. The girl had let him sleep. She'd felt sorry for him. Not only was this the first time for him, drinking had also led him to talking about his old man. James had gotten teary, telling her how much he'd loved his father; and then he'd fallen asleep. His uncle had paid for two full hours; she was going to let him take advantage of the time even if all it meant was lying next to him thinking about her own parents. Anyway, James was gentle and sweet compared to the coarse men she was used to. Earlier tonight, for instance, a miner hadn't even let her get lubricated. He'd just pushed in, hurting her. Now, like James, she closed her eyes and dozed.

The gunshot woke him. He sat straight up in bed, muttering through the mists of sleep and booze. "What happened?" James said.

Next to him in the darkness, coming awake, too, the girl said, "I don't know. I never heard no gunshot in here before. Something terrible must have happened."

Outside the door you could hear heavy boots clomping on the wooden floor; men cursing and pulling on their clothes; women saying over and over, "What happened? What happened?" as they came out of their rooms. It was like a fire drill.

James pulled on his own clothes. As he started to leave, the girl grabbed him by the wrist. "You be careful out there."

"I will."

There in the moonlight, she smiled. She sure wasn't pretty but he sure did like her. "I'm glad it was with me, the first time."

"So am I," James said, and squeezed her hand.

The hallway and the staircase were packed with retreating men. Obviously, nobody who had to make any pretense of being respectable wanted to be caught in a whorehouse. The notion now was to get the hell out of there.

On the way down the stairs, jostled in among other men, James was gawked at, pointed at, and smirked at. Old men with white hair and old men with muttonchops and old men with gold teeth peered at him wondering what the hell a fresh kid like him was doing there.

All James was concerned about was Uncle Septemus. Where was he and was he all right?

But even being pushed and shoved down the stairs by the crowd, even worried about what was going on, even sort of hungover from the alcohol . . . James was still smilingly aware of tonight's significance. It wasn't that he felt like a man exactly, it was more that he felt as if he'd learned something, that women, even ones who had to earn their living pleasing men, were every bit as real and complicated as he himself was. He'd actually liked the girl upstairs and that to him was more amazing than making love, which was wonderful and something he sure wanted to do again, but was not quite the heady mystical experience he'd assumed it would be after years of building up fantasies about it. He knew he'd never forget the girl, and not just because of the physical experience, either, but because of her rough intelligence and kindness in the face of his fears and patience in the face of his inexperience.

At the bottom of the stairs, he found his uncle.

Septemus sat in a straight-backed chair, so drunk he couldn't hold up his head, his six-shooter lying on the floor. You could smell the gun smoke, acrid even above the whiskey and perfume. The player piano was just now being turned off. Men were piling out front, side, and back doors.

The madame, a wiry little woman in a fancy blue silk dress and a hat that looked like a squatting porcupine, glared down at Uncle Septemus and said, "Who knows this sonofabitch anyway?"

"I do."

She whirled around to James.

"What'd he do, ma'm?"

"What'd he do? Why the sonofabitch started talking about some little girl gettin' killed or some god damn thing and he went crazy. Started tearin' up the room and callin' out her name and then he started firin' his gun!"

"He didn't hurt the lady, though?"

"The lady?"

"The girl he was with."

She smirked. "Ain't used to hearin' 'em called ladies." Several of the girls standing around laughed about this. "No, he didn't hurt the girl." She shook her head. Her anger went abruptly, and something like pity came into her voice. "Poor god damn bastard. Was it his daughter got killed?"

"Yes, ma'm?"

"She young?"

"Thirteen."

"Poor god damn bastard."

"Somebody shot her."

She shook her head and sighed. "Get him out of here, kid. The gunshots'll bring the sheriff and you don't want to answer a lot of questions to that sonofabitch."

James went over and got his arm under Uncle Septemus and helped him to his feet.

It was obvious Uncle Septemus had no idea where he was. Sometimes his head would roll back and he'd try to focus his brown eyes but he couldn't. Once he said "Clarice," as if she were somewhere around him and he were waiting for her.

"C'mon, kid, I'll help you," the madame said.

She got them out the back door and into the night.

There was yellow lamplight angling out the back door and making the long dusty grass green. Then the madame closed the door and everything was a rich dark prairie blue, the moon clear and round, the banking clouds gray, the elms and oaks and poplars black silhouettes against the ebony sky.

By the time he reached the street—four blocks from the hotel—the madame had turned the player piano on again. On the night air it managed to sound festive and lonely at the same time.

James dragged Uncle Septemus back to the hotel. He got sort of underneath him so Septemus could lay across his back and then he just started walking, Septemus's feet dragging in the dust. James was sweaty and winded and sore in no time but he didn't stop.

Only once did Uncle Septemus say anything. He seemed to say "Kill," and he seemed to say it two or three times. Then he was unconscious again, James taking him down alleys to avoid curious lawmen. What did Uncle Septemus mean by "kill" anyway?

Chapter Five

1

Septemus Ryan woke up at dawn. He didn't know where he was. He rolled over on the bed and looked in the gray morning light at his nephew asleep and snoring in the bed across from him. Close by roosters crowed and dogs barked. A milk wagon or a water wagon or a freight wagon jangled by in the street below. He was hot from the heat, which was already in the eighties, and also hot from his hangover. He even felt a little feverish. He'd had several hard years drinking, ever since the death of Clarice, and the drinking was taking its toll. Bloody stools, sometimes frighteningly bloody ones, from hemorrhoids that liquor only inflamed. Dry heaves in the morning sometimes, sticking his finger down his throat till the vomit came up in a hot orange gush that had a recoil like a hunting rifle. And disorientation. His employees had long ago started making jokes about his drinking, winking and smiling to each other and even shaking their heads in pity. Poor sonofabitch. Daughter's dead and he can't get over it. These days he wanted whores. He wanted them even though much of the time he was too drunk to do anything with them. He just got kind of crazy sometimes. He was always paying bills submitted to him by angry madames. Come back here and try that shit again and you god damn see what happens. He never hurt the girls. He just destroyed the rooms he was in and then usually broke down bawling. He had no idea what this was all about. He didn't care, either.

He got out of bed. James started to wake up.

"You go back to sleep now," Ryan said. "You hear me?"

But James didn't need convincing. Between the early hour and his hangover, James had barely been conscious when he'd glanced up. He fell back asleep, snoring wetly.

Ryan went down the hall to the bathroom. He filled the basin with clean tepid water that he poured from the pitcher. He washed his face and then shaved with a straight razor, getting all lathered up, and then he washed his neck and his armpits and dropped his trousers and washed his balls and his butt. He took water and a comb and got his hair to lie a certain parted way and then he was satisfied. He was a handsome man and he knew it and that was his vanity, so even on a morning such as this he wanted to look his best.

Back in the room, he put on a clean white shirt and a nice light jacket. He looked over at James only once. He smiled to himself. James would always remember last night. His first girl and most likely his first drunk. He didn't want James to be a woman and a woman was exactly what his sister was turning her son into.

The last thing he did was pick up the Winchester. Then he was ready. He left the room.

The hotel he sought was down by the tracks. The back door was flanked by garbage cans. The garbage stank, gagging sweetly like a corpse left in a hot room too long.

People weren't up and around yet. It was scarcely five A.M. Another half hour and then they'd be about their tasks.

He went up three flights of stairs to the top floor and then he went in through the fire door and halfway down the hall to room 307.

He glanced left, glanced right. Seeing nobody, he rapped on the door with one knuckle.

"God damn fucking sonofabitch," a male voice said from the other side of the door. "Who the hell is it?"

A muzzy female voice muttered something Ryan didn't understand.

Ryan rapped again. One knuckle.

"You're gonna be one sorry pecker when I get there, let me tell you," Carlyle said.

Ryan could hear covers being thrown back. Even in weather like this, some people liked covering up. He could hear Carlyle pulling his pants on. Carlyle continued to swear. The woman said nothing. Hopefully she'd gone back to sleep.

Carlyle opened the door and Ryan put the muzzle of his Winchester right in Carlyle's face.

Ryan saw that behind Carlyle the woman was still sleeping.

He got Carlyle out into the hall. The man wore pants. No socks. No shirt. He had a lot of gray chest hair and little fleshy titties like a young girl.

Ryan said, "Walk downstairs now, Carlyle. There's a buggy and you're going to get into it."

"You got the wrong man, mister," Carlyle said. It was easy to see how scared he was. It was almost disgusting to see. You'd think a man who had played a part in the death of an innocent young girl wouldn't be scared of anything.

Ryan said, "Move."

"Hey, listen," Carlyle said. "You got the wrong man. Honest."

Ryan slammed the barrel across the back of Carlye's head.

Carlyle, who appeared to be just as hungover as Ryan, started crying.

Ryan said, "Move. You understand?"

Carlyle, looking confused and baffled and imploring, snuffled some snot up into his sinuses and starting walking down the rubber runner leading to the fire door, and down the stairs outside.

Ryan made Carlyle take the reins of the top buggy. He held the Winchester on Carlyle where passersby couldn't see.

As they left town they passed the morning's first citizens, a black man washing down horses, a Mexican throwing out fry grease, and a chubby priest in a dusty black cassock sweeping off the steps of his church.

As they reached the sheriff's office, Carlyle started looking around for any sight of Dodds or his deputies. But the squat adobe building with barred windows on three sides appeared to have no one awake inside.

Carlyle looked as sad as any man Ryan had ever seen.

They rode on out of town.

"You ever have children?"

"Huh-uh."

"How come?"

"Whaddya mean how come?"

"Most men have kids."

"Just never did is all."

"Ever married?"

"Nope."

"How come?"

"What the hell you askin' me all these questions for?"

"We got a ways to go. Just trying to make the time a little more tolerable."

"You plannin' to kill me?"

"I don't know yet."

"You should look at your god damn eyes sometime, mister."

"That's enough for now," Ryan said. "Just keep your eyes on the road."

The horse was a big bay. Every ten yards or so he dropped big splashing green shit on the road. It splattered all over his fetlocks. The smell made things worse for Ryan. He shouldn't have had so much to drink last night. This morning was important.

When they got to the timber land, Ryan had Carlyle pull the wagon over.

Ryan said, waving the Winchester, "Get down."

"Get down?"

"That's what I said isn't it?"

"Why am I gettin' down?"

"Because you're going for a walk."

"You're gonna kill me, aren't you?"

"I don't know yet."

"You liar. You liar."

This time Ryan smashed the butt of the Winchester into the back of Carlyle's head. A bloody hairy hole showed on the back of Carlyle's head now.

"You sonofabitch," he said, but he got down. He held his head, trying to stop the blood, but red kept pouring between his fingers.

Ryan dug in his pocket and took out his handkerchief. "Here," he said.

Carlyle took the handkerchief and applied it to the back of his head. The white cloth turned red almost instantly. Ryan must have hit him harder than he'd thought.

"Move," Ryan said then.

"Where?"

"Into the woods. To the river."

"You sonofabitch."

But he started walking.

"You remember the dress she had on that day?" Ryan asked.

The trees were spruce and elm and maple. The shrubs were red bud and lilac and mock orange. In the underbrush were fox and rabbit and gray squirrel. You could smell the heat already. You could smell the dry dirt on the narrow winding trail through the woods. Ryan could smell the sweat and the piss on Carlyle. Ryan could smell the sleep still on himself.

After a time, them moving faster now, Ryan said, "Calico."

"Huh?"

"The dress she wore that day. Calico."

"Oh."

"She'd only worn it twice. It was her birthday dress."

"Mister, look, I—"

"You should've seen how the bullets tore up the dress. You should have seen the blood."

"God damn, mister, you got the wrong—"

"Stop. Right here."

"Mister, look—"

"I said stop."

He jammed the Winchester in Carlyle's back.

They were in a clearing. A doe stood on the edge of the long grass. Ryan could smell thistle and thyme. The deer looked so sweet he wanted to go up and hug her. Clarice at the zoo had always hugged the deer.

Ryan said, "Turn around."

"Mister—"

"Turn around."

Carlyle turned around.

"You know I'm going to kill you, don't you?"

"Mister—"

"I'm going to gut-shoot you. It's going to take a long, long time to die."

Carlyle started crying. You could smell how he'd shit his pants just then. Just standing there, just then, shit his pants.

"Mister, please—"

"There's no pleasure in this for me. I want you to know that. I'm only doing what needs to be done."

"Jesus, mister, if you'd just listen—"

Ryan put a big sopping red hole in Carlyle's stomach. There was the sound of the gunfire and the scent of gunsmoke. Carlyle's cry was a pitiful thing. He fell to the ground. He was twitching pretty bad. It was ugly to watch.

Ryan walked over and stood next to him. Ryan looked down and said, "You should've seen that calico dress, Carlyle. You should've seen it."

Carlyle was sobbing. Ryan could see every piece of beard stubble on Carlyle's chin and every whiskey and tobacco stain on his teeth. "Holy Mary, Mother of God," Carlyle was saying, praying out loud without any kind of shame at all.

Ryan watched him for a time. Stood there. Just watching.

After a time the convulsions started.

"Shit, mister, just shoot me. Please. Jesus, please. Please."

The blood soaked into his trousers now. You could see life fading in the blue eyes. Fading.

"Please," he said. "I can't take it no more. Please."

Ryan lifted the Winchester and pointed it directly at Carlyle's face. He didn't have the taste for torture after all. He put the weapon right on Carlyle's nose. "You sure you want it this way?"

Carlyle was in so much pain he couldn't even talk. All he could do was nod. His lips were already dry and white and chapped.

"You should've seen what that calico looked like," Ryan said.

Ryan shot him in the face. He blew his nose off. All that remained was a ragged hole with blood chugging out. Ryan stared until he couldn't stand to stare any longer.

A jay came and sat on Carlyle's forehead and pointed a delicate beak at the hole in the dead man's face and started tasting the blood. Already you could see plump black ants coming up.

Ryan took one more look at Carlyle then hefted his Winchester and left.

2

"Morning, Mrs. Griff."

"Morning, Sheriff."

"Wondered if your husband would be around?"

"'Fraid not. He went over town early."

Dodds smiled. "Darned early. It's hardly seven."

"He was needin' some kind of wrench he didn't have. Said he could borrow one from Charlie Smythe."

Dodds nodded to the barn in back. "He still works on his buggies, huh?"

"They're his pride and joy."

"Guess they would be," Dodds said. "He built some good ones when the wagon works was open." Seeing that he'd made Mrs. Griff melancholy—he was not what you'd call steeped in the social graces, particularly where women were concerned—he bent down to look more closely at the two little girls who stood on either side of their mother. "Now let me see. One of you is Eloise and one of you is Tess. Right?"

The older girl giggled and blush. "Uh-huh, Sheriff, uh-huh."

"You'd be Eloise, wouldn't you? The oldest one?"

"Uh-huh."

"How old are you, sweetie?"

"I'm six and Tess is four."

"Four!" Dodds said, turning to the littlest girl. She had golden braids—her sister had dark hair—and wore a blue calico dress. "Why, I thought you were five for sure."

Tess blushed and buried her face in her mother's apron. Dodds looked up at Mrs. Griff and winked. "Last time I saw your mother, I said that, didn't I, Mrs. Griff? I said why I thought that Tess was five years old for sure."

The girls giggled and flushed some more, thoroughly charmed.

Dodds straightened up, his bones cracking as he did so. The older one got, the more noises one's body made. "Do you suppose you could walk me down to the corner, Mrs. Griff? Maybe have Eloise and Tess stay here?"

He could see the instant alarm in the woman's eyes. He hadn't wanted to put it there but there was no other way.

"Why don't you girls go back and finish your breakfast," Mrs.

Griff said. He could hear the tightness in her voice, the fear. Something was wrong and now she knew it. She was a plump woman, but pretty even though her hair had started turning gray. She had always struck Dodds as one of those women who can handle any crisis, much stronger than most men at such moments, himself included. But now, panic besetting her gaze and sweet pink mouth, he saw her vulnerability. He was almost disappointed.

They set out down the walk.

"Just tell me straight out," she said. He could feel her trying to remain calm.

"I think he's in some trouble, Mrs. Griff."

"What kind of trouble?"

"Old trouble, actually. A bank robbery a few years back."

"A bank robbery?" She smiled with a kind of pretty bitterness. "Believe me, Sheriff, you go take a look at the food on our table and then you tell me that we ever saw any money from a bank robbery."

"That was one of the problems, at least from the robbers' point of view. A young girl got killed and the robbers got all het up and took off without any money."

"A young girl?"

"Thirteen. Delivering something to the bank for her father."

"My Lord." She sounded shocked and almost angry. Obviously she was thinking of her own girls.

They walked a time in silence. Kids were invading the green dusty summer day, streaming clean from the small white respectable houses of Tencourt Street, eager to soil shirts and trousers and dresses and, most especially, faces.

"Why do you think my husband had anything to do with this?"

"An ex-Pinkerton man was in town a while back. He'd traced the robbers to here."

"And he said Mike was one of them?"

"That's what he said."

"Who else?"

"He said Kittredge and Carlyle."

At the last name her face turned sour with a frown. "Carlyle, I could understand. But not Mike or Kittredge. They're good men, Sheriff, and you know it." She was watching him now, expecting him to agree.

"That they are, Mike and Dennis," he said. "Good men. But think back to when the wagon works closed. Think how desperate men were around here." He didn't have the courage to look at her as he said this.

They reached the corner. A small band of kids stood ten feet away pointing at the sheriff, or more specifically at his badge. It always brought a lot of ooohs and aaahs of the sort kids muster for people in uniform.

Now they faced each other and Dodds said, "The girl's father came to town yesterday."

"My God. Does he think Mike is responsible?"

"I'm pretty sure that's what he thinks."

"Are you going to tell him otherwise?"

This was the hard part for Dodds. "Mrs. Griff, I'd like you to talk to Mike and have him turn himself in at my office."

"My God. You think he did it, don't you?"

"I'm afraid I do."

"My God."

"If he don't turn himself in, Mrs. Griff, he's at the mercy of this fellow Ryan. So far Ryan has done nothing I can arrest him for. That means he'll have every opportunity to kill the three men." He hesitated a minute. "You'd rather have Mike alive, wouldn't you?"

"He couldn't have killed a girl. He just couldn't have."

"It was an accident. Even the bank employees agree on that. An accident. So in all likelihood he wouldn't be facing any murder charge. Least not a first degree one." His jaw clamped. "You've got to see this Ryan fellow to know what I'm talking about, Mrs. Griff. He's insane. He's so grieved over his daughter that nothing else matters than killing the men responsible. If Mike don't turn himself in, Mrs. Griff, Ryan's gonna kill him for sure."

"My God," she said.

The kids watching them inched closer. One kid said, "Sheriff, did your badge really cost two hunnerd dollars?"

The sheriff winked at Mrs. Griff and said to the kid, "Oh, a lot more than that, Frankie. You just can't see the jewels I got on the other side."

"Jewels! Wow! See, I tole ya!" Frankie said to the other kid and then they took off running, tumbling into the morning.

"You tell Mike to turn himself in, Mrs. Griff," Dodds said after turning back to the woman. "That's the safest way for everybody." He touched her elbow. "Please do it, Mrs. Griff. I don't want anybody else to die because of all this. The girl was enough."

Mrs. Griff was crying now; soft silver tears in her soft gray eyes. "He just couldn't have killed any girl, Sheriff," she said. "Not on purpose; not on purpose." That's all she could think of, the girl.

"You tell him," Dodds said quietly. "Please, Mrs. Griff. All right?"

He went back to his office.

3

The hangover felt like a fever in James, but not so much a fever that he couldn't think about the girl last night. He was changed, and this morning the change felt even more important than it had last night. He wished he had a good male friend in Council Bluffs, somebody you could really talk to—partly to impress, of course (not many boys his age had ever actually slept with a girl), and partly just as a confidant. Obviously he couldn't tell his mother and he couldn't tell Marietta. And his uncle already knew about it and . . .

His uncle. James looked across at the empty bed. Apparently Septemus had gotten dressed and gone downstairs for breakfast. James thought about last night. It was pretty sad, really, Septemus getting so drunk and sort of shooting up the place and then starting to cry. James thought about what his mother had said of Septemus ever since Clarice had died. How his uncle wasn't quite right somehow . . .

For the twenty minutes James had been awake, shoes and boots and bare feet could be heard passing by on the other side of the door. Every time he'd think it was his uncle, the sound would move on down the hall. So, lying there now, he held out no hope that the sounds of leather squeaking would actually be his uncle. But the door opened abruptly and in came Septemus.

"Good morning, James!" Septemus said, striding in and shutting the door behind him. "Are you ready for a big breakfast? I certainly am."

James rolled off the bed and started getting into his clothes. He kept looking at Septemus. Despite the good cheer of his booming voice, there was something wrong with Septemus. He couldn't look James in the face.

"Then we'll go for a ride," Septemus said, rummaging for something in his carpetbag.

James saw Septemus take his Navy Colt from the bag, open his coat, and put the weapon inside his belt. Then he closed the coat again.

"You ready, son?"

"Mind if I wash up?"

"Of course not, James."

Septemus slapped James on the back. He would still not let his eyes meet James's.

"Uncle Septemus?"

"Yes, James?"

"Is something wrong?"

"Wrong? Why would you say a thing like that? Look out the window. It's a fine morning. And listen to all the wagons in the street below. It's not only a fine morning, it's a busy morning. The sounds of commerce, that's what you hear in the street below. The sound of commerce." His voice was good-naturedly booming again. But then why were his eyes filled with tears?

Something was terribly wrong. James wondered what it could be.

"I'll be right back," James said, and went down the hall.

A man was coming out of the bathroom just as James was ready to go in. The smell the man had left behind was so sour James had to hold his breath while he poured fresh water into the basin and got himself all scrubbed up.

When he was all through, he stared at himself in the mirror with his hair combed and a clean collar on.

Yes, he definitely looked older. Seventeen, maybe; or even eighteen. He had to thank Uncle Septemus for taking him along last night.

But when he thought of Uncle Septemus, he thought of his strange mood this morning. Where had Septemus gone so early in the day? And why was he putting on this blustery act of being so happy? Septemus hadn't been a happy man even before the murder of his daughter; afterward, he'd been inconsolable.

When he got back to the room he saw Septemus sitting on the edge of the bed staring at the rotogravure of Clarice he carried everywhere with him.

"She was a fine girl," his uncle said.

"She sure was."

Septemus looked up at him. "You miss her a lot, don't you, James?"

"Yes, I do."

Septemus continued to stare at him. "It changed all our lives, didn't it, when she was killed, I mean?"

James thought a moment. He felt guilty that he could not answer honestly. Sure, he was sad when Clarice had died, and he did indeed think about her pretty often. But change his life? Not really; not in the way his uncle meant. "Yes; yes it did."

"You're a good boy, James."

"Thank you."

"Or excuse me. After last night, you're a boy no longer. You're half a man."

"Half?"

Septemus's troubled brown eyes remained on his. "There's one more thing you need to learn. You know firsthand about carnality, and the pleasures only a woman can render a man, but now you need to learn about the opposite of pleasure."

"The opposite of pleasure?"

"Responsibility. You have to pay for the pleasures of being a man by taking on the responsibilities of a man."

James noticed how Septemus had gone back to staring at the picture.

"What responsibilities?"

Septemus put the picture back in his carpetbag then stood up, putting on the good mood again. "Come on now, young man, we're going down to the restaurant and have the finest breakfast they've ever served."

James couldn't quell his appetite, even while he was beginning to worry about what Septemus must have in mind for them today.

"Bacon and eggs and hash browns," Septemus said as they strolled down the hall. "How does that sound?"

"It sounds great."

"And with lots of strawberry marmalade spread all over hot bread."

James could barely keep himself from salivating. In the onslaught of such food, he gradually forgot about Septemus's ominous talk of responsibility.

4

She had sat at the kitchen table rehearsing what she would say to him. How easy it was when it was words spoken only to herself, only in her mind.

Be honest with me, Mike. Whatever you've done, tell me, and I'll stand by you. I know you couldn't have killed that young girl, so tell me your side of things, Mike. Let me hear the honest truth from you.

Then she saw him coming up the walk, the girls hurling themselves at him so he'd pick them up in his strong callused hands and strong muscular arms and carry them inside.

The three of them came bursting through the door, the girls laughing because he was tickling them. He set them down and Tess said, "He said I was five years old, Daddy."

"Who said?" Griff said, tickling her again.

"The sheriff."

"The sheriff?" Griff said, fluffing her blond hair. "Was he trying to arrest you?"

Tess nodded to her mother. "He came here to see Mommy."

Griff's face tightened. "Dodds came here?"

His wife said, "Yes."

"When?"

"Not long after you walked overtown."

"What did he want?"

She scooched the girls outdoors.

"How come we have to go outside, Mommy?" Tess said.

"Because it's summer and that's where little girls are supposed to be. Outside."

She closed the door and turned around. Griff was pouring himself a cup of coffee from the pot on the stove. No matter how hot it got, Griff always liked steaming coffee.

He went over and sat at the kitchen table. "What did he say?"

She decided against any sort of coyness or hesitation. "He said you were in trouble."

"He say what kind?"

"There was a bank robbery. A young girl was killed."

He stared at her a long time. "You believe that?"

"I'm not sure. Not about the girl, I mean. I know you well enough to know you could never hurt a child."

"How about the bank?"

She came over and sat down across from him at the table. The oilcloth smelled pleasant. "He said it was right after the wagon works closed. I remember what you were like in those days. Desperate. You thought we might lose the house and everything."

"What if I told you that I did help rob that bank?"

"I'd do my best to understand."

"What if I told you that the girl dying was a pure accident?"

"I'd believe that, too."

"Dodds tell you that the girl's father is here?"

"Yes. He says the man means to kill you."

He met her gaze. He looked sad and tense. "Can't say I blame him, can you?"

"It was an accident."

"What if it was Eloise or Tess? Would you be so forgiving just because it was an accident?"

"I reckon not."

"Dodds going to come and arrest me?"

"He wants you to turn yourself in."

"How do you feel about that?"

"I wish you would."

"It'd mean prison."

"I've thought about that, Mike."

"Not all women want to wait for their men."

She touched his coarse strong hand. "I love you, Mike. You made a mistake but that doesn't take away any of my feelings for you."

"I don't think I could tolerate prison. I'm too old. Too used to my freedom."

"What's the alternative?"

"Let this man Ryan try something. Then Dodds will have to run him in."

"Won't Dodds turn on you then?"

"He doesn't have any evidence. He just has the word of this ex-Pinkerton man who was through here a while back."

She put her head down and said a quick prayer for guidance. Then she raised her head and smiled at him. "The girls and I'll come see you. Every week if they'll let us."

"It'd be a terrible life for you."

"We'd get by."

He stared out the back window at the barn where his buggies

were. She could tell he was thinking about them. Next to the girls and herself, the buggies were his abiding pride. He picked up his steaming coffee and blew on the hot liquid and said, "Let me think about it a little while."

She touched his hand again. "I love you, Mike. And so do the girls. Just remember that."

His eyes left the window and turned back to her. "I don't know what the hell I ever did to deserve you, but I sure am a lucky man."

She laughed and there were tears in her laugh. "You expect me to disagree with that?"

Then he laughed, too, and went back to staring out the window at the buggies.

5

"Your father coming back?"

James smiled up at the waiter. "Oh, he's not my father."

"Well, I certainly noticed a resemblance, young man."

"I suppose it's because he's my uncle."

"Uncle, is it?" the waiter asked. He had a gray walrus mustache and a thick head of wavy gray hair. His short black jacket was spotless and the serving tray he bore was shiny stainless steel. He also had a heavy brogue. "Uncle would explain it."

"He left this," James said, and slid the bill and several greenbacks to the edge of the table.

The waiter fingered the money with the skill of a pickpocket. "I'll be bringin' you your change," he said, though given the slight hesitation in his voice, James knew that the man hoped there would be no change.

"He said it was all for you."

The waiter laughed hoarsely. "Well, now, isn't that a way to gladden a man's day?" He offered James a small bow. "And I hope your day is gladdened, too, young one."

"Thank you."

"And thank you," the waiter said, and left.

In half an hour a rented wagon was to pull up in front of the restaurant and James was to go out and meet it. Septemus said he would be driving. He said that James should come out fast and jump up and ask no questions. His appetite sated, his hangover waning, he had started wondering again exactly what his uncle was doing.

Why the wagon? Why come out fast? Why ask no questions?

He put his chin in the palm of his hand and stared out the window at the dusty street filled with pedestrians walking from one side to the other. He started thinking again of last night, of what he'd done with the girl, and he decided that the first thing he was going to do when he got back to Council Bluffs was get himself a good friend so he'd have somebody to tell about his experiences.

Then he started thinking of Uncle Septemus's comment that James was only half a man, that only when he took "responsibility" would he be a full man.

James started wondering where Uncle Septemus was right then.

6

In the lobby, Dodds went over to the desk and asked if Septemus Ryan was in his room.

The clerk shook his head. "Saw both him and his nephew go out a while ago." The clerk wore a drummer's striped shirt and a pitiful scruffy little mustache and had a lot of slick goop on his rust-colored hair. He was the Hames's eldest, nineteen years old or so, and this was his first job in town. As far as Dodds was concerned he took it far too seriously. The only law and order the kid respected was that of Mel Lutz who owned the hotel and two other businesses.

"I'm going up to their room." He put out his hand. "I'd appreciate the key."

"Sheriff, now you know what Judge Mason said. He said you shouldn't ought to do that unless you check with him first. 'Bout how people had rights and all. And anyway Mel says I shouldn't ought to do it unless I check with him first."

"He in his office?"

"Yup."

"Then go check an' I'll wait here."

"What about the judge?"

"The judge'll be my concern. Now you go talk to Mel."

"Who'll watch the desk?"

"I'll watch the desk."

"I ain't sure that'd be right."

"What the hell you think I'm gonna do, boy-kid, steal somethin'?"

"No offense, Sheriff, but you ain't one of Mel's employees. And Mel's rule is that only a bona fide employee can be behind the desk."

"Boy, I just happen to be sheriff of this here burg. Now if that don't qualify me to be behind that desk, what does?"

"Guess that's a fair point."

"Now you go tell Mel I want the key."

"Can I tell him why you want the key?"

Dodds sighed. "'Cause I want to go up there and look around."

"Can I tell him why you want to go up there and look around?"

"Kid, you're lucky I don't punch you right on the nose."

"I'm just askin' the questions Mel's gonna ask me."

"I think Ryan's up to somethin' and I want to see if I can get some kind of evidence on him."

The kid leaned forward on his elbow and said, "What's he up to?"

"Git, now. Go ask Mel. That's all I'm gonna say."

The kid stood up, frowning. Obviously disappointed. Like most desk clerks, the kid was a gold-plated gossip.

"Git," the sheriff said.

The kid got.

In all, Dodds leaned on the desk for ten minutes while the kid was away. He said hello to maybe twenty people, sent icy stares at a couple of others he suspected of being confidence men working the area, and helped three different ladies out the front door with their packages.

Dodds liked the hotel's lobby, the leather furnishings, the ferns, the hazy air of cigar and pipe smoke, the bright brass cuspidors, the seemingly endless pinochle game that went on over in the corner. This was where the town's men spent their retirement years. Didn't matter if they were married or not, they always came down there. It was almost like working a shift at a factory. The missus made breakfast and then one took a morning walk and ended up at the hotel. The first thing to do was sit in one of the plump leather chairs and read the paper and then discuss any pressing politics and any pressing town gossip and then help oneself to the pinochle game. Dodds was a piss-poor pinochle player. He would have to get one hell of a lot better before he retired.

"Here's the key, Sheriff," the kid said when he came back. "Mel said five minutes."

"So he's setting time limits now, is he?"

"I'm only tellin' you what he tole me, Sheriff."

Dodds took the key. "Thanks, kid."

The kid held up the five fingers of his left hand and pointed to them with the index finger of his right hand. "Remember, Mel said five minutes."

Dodds restrained himself from telling the kid what an aggravating bastard he could be.

Dodds had always liked hotels. He liked the idea of all the different kinds of people and different kinds of lives being led in them. After his wife died, he'd thought of giving up the small house they'd lived in and moving in to the hotel. He still thought about it, about taking three meals downstairs at a long table covered with a fresh white linen cloth every time, sitting up in his room with a cigar and a magazine and a rocker and watching the sunset and listening to people on their way into the festive night, just sitting there smelling of shaving soap and hair oil, clean as a whistle and without a care.

He thought of all these things as he moved along the corridor to Ryan's room. Taking no chances, he pulled out his revolver, put an ear to the door, and listened. That kid desk clerk could easily have missed Ryan coming back up to his room. Or hell, maybe for some reason Ryan snuck up the back way.

He tried the door knob. Locked. He took out the key, fit it into the lock, and turned it.

He'd been in these rooms many times. In the daylight they looked somewhat shabby. The paint had faded, some of the wallpaper had worked free, the brass beds were getting a little rusty, and the linoleum was pretty scuffed up.

The first carpetbag he tried belonged to the kid. Or at least he assumed it did, unless a grown man carried a slingshot and a Buffalo Bill novel.

In the second carpetbag he found the newspaper stories. There were ten in all, clipped carefully from the front pages of newspapers around the state, some with pictures, some not. It was the same terrible story again and again, the thirteen-year-old girl slain during the bank robbery, the huge rewards offered for the capture of the men, the grieving father and the outrage of the townspeople.

Dodds also found the letter.

The thing ran three pages on a fancy buff blue stock and it was written in a fine, clear longhand that managed to be both attractive and masculine. It said just about what one would expect such a letter to say. While reading it, Dodds kept thinking of Ryan's brown eyes, forlorn and angry and mad all at the same time.

Dodds had to smile about who the letter was addressed to—it was addressed to him. Ryan had thought of everything. He would come to Myles and do what he wanted and, when it was done, Dodds would have the letter for explanation as to who had done it and why it had been done and what was to be made of it in the common mind.

Shaking his head, Dodds tucked the letter back inside the

unsealed envelope, put the letter back inside the carpetbag, and left the room. He moved very quickly for a man his age.

If he didn't find Ryan fast things were going to get real bad in town. Real bad.

Chapter Six

1

There was something wrong with a man in his forties sitting in a small, crowded confessional telling the priest that not only had he taken the Lord's name in vain, not only had he missed mass several times in the past few months, but also that he'd defiled himself. That was the term Kittredge had been taught, "defiled." Kittredge had a prostate problem. The damn thing got boggy as a rotten apple. This was because of Mae, of course; ever since Mae had miscarried, she'd shown little interest in sex, and Kittredge never felt like forcing himself on her. He felt sorry enough for her as it was, what with the sheets a bloody mess that night and Mae not quite right about anything ever since. He'd tried whorehouses twice but afterward he felt disgusted with himself. There he was liquored up and laughing with some woman who had no morals at all and there was Mae at home in the shadows of their little house, her hands all rosary-wrapped and her gaze fixed far away on something Kittredge had never been able to see.

Earlier this morning, just after waking, the day in the open window smelling of impending rain, these were the thoughts Kittredge had.

Soon after, he went downstairs and scrubbed and shaved for the day. He took the clothes Mae had set out for him and tugged them on and then went into the kitchen where she had two eggs, two strips of bacon, and a big slice of toast waiting for him. She sat across from him, watching him as he ate. This always seemed to give her a peculiar satisfaction he could not understand but found endearing. She would have looked even more fondly at their child eating, he knew. Maybe that's what she pretended, watching him this way, that he was their child.

"You got any special plans today?" she said.

"Sloane says there's no work. Thought I might go down by the creek and do some fishing. Maybe I can catch us something for tonight."

She smiled, watched him stand up and go to the door. "Maybe I'll bake us a cake."

"Now I know I'm gonna have to catch us a fish."

"A chocolate cake with white frosting."

It was his favorite kind. He walked back to her and took her face tenderly in his hands and kissed her gently on the lips. "You're a good woman, Mae."

"You keep on tellin' me that often enough, Dennis, I'm likely to start believin' it."

This time he kissed her on the forehead.

* * *

Two hours in, he'd caught nothing. He sat on a piece of lime-stone. The day was hot but overcast. The water was cloudy. A wild dog came by and tried to steal the lunch he'd brought along but he shooed it away, though for a few moments there the damn animal had scared him some. The county had been infested with rabies just a year ago and doctors everywhere were warning folks to be careful.

His favorite time to fish was autumn, when the days were gold and red and brown with fall colors and the nights were silver with frost. Then he worked fyke nets and basket traps and moved down-river in his johnboat where he made driftwood fires to keep warm. The autumn embraced him and held him in a way furious summer did not. There was solace in autumn and in summer none.

Ryan pulled the buggy into a copse of poplars. The soil there was red and sandy, the bunch grass brown from heat. His hangover was still pretty bad. He had to stop every mile or so to pee, and he kept thinking he had to vomit. The food hadn't helped all that much.

He left the Winchester in the buggy and set off across the woods to Kittredge's house.

Almost immediately after he knocked, a small, worn-looking woman came to the door.

"Mrs. Kittredge?"

"Yes."

"I'm Special Deputy Forbes."

"Special deputy?"

He knew instantly she was alarmed. It was just what he wanted her to be.

"I need to speak with your husband."

"With Dennis?"

"Yes."

"Has he done something wrong.?"

Ryan shook his head. "Not at all, ma'm. Not at all. He may have seen something the other day and we need to get his testimony."

"Seen something?" She still sounded suspicious, wary.

"An incident in town." Ryan smiled. Now he wanted her to ease up some, relax. "Something was taken from the jewelry store. We're told your husband was standing in the middle of the street at that time. He may have seen the thief."

"Which jewelry store would that be? I didn't know we had no jewelry store."

It was Ryan's intention to remain calm. He inhaled sharply, put the smile back on his face, and said, "Forgive me, ma'm, I'm down from the state capital so I'm not all that familiar with the town here."

But she wasn't trying to trap him. In fact, she helped him out of his dilemma. "Ragan's sells jewelry. That's the general store. They keep some jewelry in the back. Maybe you mean Ragan's.

"That's exactly what I mean. That's exactly the name the sheriff used."

He saw her face slacken, the heavy worry lines fading some. She shook her head. He thought he even detected a small, oddly bitter smile. "Wouldn't that be just Dennis's luck?"

"Ma'm?"

"Goes over town on a completely innocent errand and gets himself mixed up in some kind of robbery."

"I see."

"No offense, but you know how it is when you get tied up goin' to court and everything."

"Yes, ma'm, that's one thing I'm very familiar with."

"Poor Dennis. He won't be happy to hear that."

"No, ma'm."

"But I s'pose it's his civic duty."

"Yes, ma'm." He paused and said, "Where might I find him, ma'm?"

"He went fishing."

"Do you happen to know where?"

"He's got a favorite spot just north of here. Up near the bluffs." She pointed in the direction of ragged clay hills. "He'll probably be back in a few hours."

"Oh, I'm sure I can find him, ma'm."

Wariness showed in her eyes again. "You seem to be in a pretty big hurry to talk to him."

"Just like to get this settled so I can head back on the evening train."

"And you say you're a special deputy?"

"That's right, ma'm."

"Working with the sheriff?'

"Yes, ma'm. Down from the capital to help on the jewelry investigation."

"Never heard of such a thing."

Ryan smiled again. "It's an election year, ma'm."

"Election year?"

Ryan nodded. "The governor makes his special deputies available to anybody who asks."

"I see."

"Good politics, ma'm."

The suspicion died in her voice again. "I suppose." She put her face up into the air the way a small dog might. "You can smell rain coming. Dennis'll probably get soaked." She nodded to Ryan. "You tell him I'm working on that cake I promised him."

"I'll tell him, ma'm."

She gave him a curious look, then. "And tell . . . tell him I'm thinking about him."

Ryan knew that she really wanted to say "Tell him I love him," but that she was too inhibited. Somehow she knew, Ryan saw; knew what was really going on, much as she tried denying it to herself.

Ryan tipped his hat. "Good luck with that cake, ma'm."

But she was still giving him that curious, wary gaze. She didn't say good-bye. She just nodded and wiped her hands on her apron again and went back inside the house, closing the door behind her.

By the time Ryan went over the hill to his buggy, the first drops of rain had begun to fall. Plump, clear drops that were hot against the skin. He wished he hadn't liked the Kittredge woman as much as he had. He felt sorry for her. What he was about to do would destroy her life forever. He wished she could have been mean or stupid or offensive in some way.

He got in the buggy and started up the dusty trail that wound into the red clay foothills.

He kept thinking of the Kittredge woman. Maybe because he saw some of his own sorrow in her. They were not unalike, the two of them. Maybe that was it.

2

Half an hour later, the rain was coming down hot and slow. Black clouds covered the already faint sun. It was dark as dusk and the temperature had dropped ten degrees. Coming up over the clay cliffs, Ryan smelled how the rain stirred up the dust and gave it a chalky odor.

He leaned against a poplar and looked down at the bank below. The creek was wide there, deep and fast enough to look treacherous for animals, and the water hitting the surface of it made wide, soft circles.

He hefted the Winchester, aimed, and shot the hat directly off the head of Dennis Kittredge.

Kittredge put on a little show. Knowing that there was nowhere to hide, that he was several precious yards from either boulders or trees, he pitched himself to the right and started rolling in the dust.

Ryan put another shot a few feet ahead of where Kittredge was about to light.

This time Kittredge let out a crazed animal yelp. A fella didn't like to think that circumstances were completely beyond his control, but obviously they now were.

"Just stand up, Mr. Kittredge," Ryan said, starting down the slope, keeping the Winchester right on Ryan's chest. "That way you're not likely to get shot."

Kittredge got to his feet. His fishing pole had rolled off the bank and dropped into the water.

"What the hell do you think you're doing?" Kittredge said. Unlike Carlyle, Kittredge didn't seem so much frightened as angry. He was casual enough to dust off his trousers.

Ryan didn't answer. He came down the clay to the bank and then put the Winchester in Kittredge's face.

"You know why I'm here, Mr. Kittredge."

" I know why you say you're here. I talked to Carlyle. He said you think we had something to do with a bank robbery."

Ryan smiled. "We're beyond pretenses, Mr. Kittredge. I'd say ask Carlyle, but I'm afraid you can't do that. Not anymore."

"What's that supposed to mean?"

"It means he's dead."

For the first time, some of Kittredge's anger waned and something resembling fear narrowed his eyes and pulled his face tight. "You kill him, Ryan?"

"I did."

Kittredge didn't say anything.

Ryan said, "You should've seen it. He was pleading with me to do it."

"I don't want to hear about it."

"He was on the ground and I put the rifle hard against his nose."

"He didn't have that coming."

Ryan considered him a long time. "It's my understanding you don't have any children, Mr. Kittredge. It's my understanding that your wife can't bear you any."

Kittredge glared at him.

"Then you can't appreciate what it is to lose a child. Oh, I know that you *think* you can, Mr. Kittredge. But believe me, until you see your child—"

He didn't finish the sentence.

Thunder rumbled across the sky; lightning trembled gold and silver beneath black clouds. The rain fell in stead, monotonous drops.

Ryan said, "Anyway, Mr. Kittredge, it's not something you can imagine. It's something you have to experience." He smiled at Kittredge. "You know what my daughter's very last words were to me,

Mr. Kittredge? I'll never forget. She came up to me from the back of the store and said, 'Daddy, I'd like to take the bank deposit over now. Then I'm going to stop and pick you a bouquet of flowers because I love you so much.' Those were her very last words, Mr. Kittredge."

Kittredge let his gaze fall to his feet.

Ryan said, "She never did get to pick me those flowers, Mr. Kittredge. I keep wondering what kind she would have gotten me." He looked at Kittredge and smiled again. "What kind do you think she would have gotten me, Mr. Kittredge?"

Kittredge said nothing. He would not look up.

"You think she would have brought me roses, Mr. Kittredge?"

Nothing.

"Or maybe daisies."

Nothing.

"You going to answer me, Mr. Kittredge?"

Kittredge shuffled his feet. Still he said nothing.

"Seems to me an intelligent man could make an intelligent guess about what kind of flowers she would pick for her father, Mr. Kittredge. Roses or daisies or zinnias."

Kittredge's head came up slowly. He looked at Ryan for a long time.

Kittredge said, "I'm sorry your little girl died, Ryan."

"You didn't answer my question."

"I really am sorry."

"Do you think she would have picked roses for me, Mr. Kittredge?"

"This won't bring her back. Killin' Carlyle or killin' me. It won't bring her back, Ryan. It won't bring her back."

Ryan hit him so hard with the butt of the rifle that Kittredge easily went over backward, his arms flailing all the way down.

Ryan went over to him then and kicked him once, hard in the face. You could hear his nose shatter and splatter. Right away the bleeding was bad.

Ryan said, "If you think I'm going to get it over with fast, the way I did with Carlyle, you're wrong, Mr. Kittredge. Carlyle didn't have the brains of a rock. But you—you and Griff—you're smart men, responsible men. So you've got a special price to pay and you're going to pay it."

Through a very bloody mouth, his eyes wild now the way Carlyle's had been, Kittredge said, "I'm sorry about your little girl, Ryan. I really am."

This time Ryan kicked him hard on the side of the face, along the jawline.

Kittredge rolled into the dirt, facedown. He made moaning and sobbing sounds.

The rain hit Kittredge's back so hard it sounded like bullets being absorbed by the flesh.

The creek rattled with rain now.

Ryan stood over Kittredge and then finally he took the rope from his pocket.

Ryan said, "Here you go, Mr. Kittredge. Here you go."

3

By this time James was beginning to think his uncle had forgotten him. James had been sitting in the restaurant for two hours now, looking and watching out the rain-streaked window, and he was beginning to feel like a little boy kept indoors by a spring downpour.

Every ten minutes or so the hostess would come around and ask if he wanted another spafizz but James would only shake his head and smile bleakly.

Then he would turn resolutely back to the window, expecting his uncle to be there suddenly, like a gift left on a doorstep.

It was while he was watching that he saw the girl across the street trip on the boardwalk and go falling to her knees in the mud. Her parasol went flying into the path of a wagon. The horses trampled right over it. The girl, not one to take such a slight politely, raised her tiny fist and shook it in the direction of the retreating wagon.

Several of the older male customers inside the restaurant had also watched this little nickelodeon adventure played out in the rain and mud. They rubbed their muttonchops and patted the plump bellies they'd covered with silk vests and pointed to the girl.

One man said, "It's that young whore Liz."

Looking into the street again, James saw that it was indeed the girl he'd spent much of last night with.

Another stout man laughed. "A little mud never hurt a girl like that."

Liz obliged her oglers by starting to stand up, mud clinging to her hands and arms and the whole of her skirt, and promptly falling right back down to her knees.

The men in the restaurant began poking each other and pointing out of the window as if they were spectators at a particularly funny play.

"Too bad she doesn't put on a show when you go up to see her," one man laughed.

James, disliking the meanness and arrogance of the men, got up from his chair and started running down the aisle to the door. He tromped hard on one man's shoes as he fled out the door, stomping down directly on the instep. This was the man who'd referred to Liz as a "young whore." The man cursed James and shook a fat fist in the boy's direction.

The rain pelted him immediately. It was a cold rain and hard. It was also difficult to see through.

He waded out into the street that had become a vast mud puddle. He sank in halfway to his knees. The mud made faint sucking sounds as he raised and lowered his feet.

He noticed that several people stood on the boardwalk under the overhang pointing to Liz and smirking much as the men in the restaurant had. It was obvious they knew who she was and what she was and would make no move to help her. The women twirling their parasols and peering out from beneath their picture hats looked particularly mean.

The street was so swampy it took him two full minutes to reach her. By this time she had fallen over yet again, and now even her face was mud-spattered.

She didn't recognize him at first. She was obviously angry and hurt and ashamed and so instead of thanking this helpful stranger, she tried to slap him.

The people along the boardwalk started laughing again.

James took the hand she meant to slap him with and said, "Don't you remember me, Liz?"

There in the drenching rain, there in the echoes of the crowd's harsh laughter, she narrowed her eyes and looked more closely at him. "You're the kid from last night."

He noted how she said that. She had not called him by name. There had been no warmth or even surprise in her voice. She was simply identifying him.

He said, above the rain, "I had a nice time last night."

She shook her head. "Kid, just help me get out of here, will you?"

But he felt hurt. "Didn't you have a nice time.?"

Now she shouted above the rain. "Maybe you didn't notice but they're starting to laugh at you, too."

"Let them," he said. "I just want to know if you had a good time last night."

"I had a great time."

"You don't sound as if you mean that, Liz."

There in the rain, them both shouting, both soaked and mud-mired, she leaned over and kissed him on the cheek and said, "You know something, kid? You really are a kid. A sweet one."

The crowd found this even more wonderful entertainment. A few of them even applauded.

"Will you help me get across the street to the boardwalk?" Liz said.

He slid his arm in hers. "I'd be proud to."

She smiled at him uncertainly. "You haven't been drinking again today, have you, kid?"

He smiled back. "Not so far."

They walked across the street, step by inching step. By now James was mud-soaked, too.

Once, she fell and he had to help her up. Once, he fell and she had to help him up. The crowd loved it.

"They really make me mad," James said as they drew near the boardwalk.

"Why?"

"Because of how they treat you."

She stopped and stared at him through the silver rain. "Kid, I'm a whore. How do you expect them to treat me?"

"You should have more pride in yourself than that."

She squeezed his arm and smiled again.

Now he smiled. "And stop calling me kid. I'm nearly two years older than you."

So they resumed their walk.

Now it was apparent they were going to make it without further incident, the crowd began to disperse. Their entertainment was over.

When they finally reached the protection of the overhang, she began to look herself over, shaking her head. "No wonder they was laughin'."

"Why?"

"I ain't real pretty on the best of days. Lookin' like this . . ." She shook her head again. Her hair was formed against her head like the sculpted hair of a statue.

"Who said you aren't pretty?"

She had been scraping mud from her skirts. She stopped and looked up at him. "Kid, I don't think I can take any more of your chivalry."

"But Liz, I'm just trying to be—"

"I know what you're trying to be!" she said. She glanced over at two townsmen standing there watching her. Smirking. "Kid, sometimes being nice hurts worse than anything else. Because I'm not used to people being nice to me."

And he saw then in her tears and heard in the stricken sound of her voice the pain and dread she tried not to acknowledge.

"Kid, just go be nice to somebody else, all right?"

And then she left, her footsteps sharp against the wood of the boardwalk, a muddy little farm girl aging too quickly in the harsh city.

"Don't worry, son," one of the onlookers said. "There's plenty more back at that house where she came from."

James felt as if he wanted to take a swing at the guy, but it was just then that a male voice shouted his name through the rain, and he turned to see, standing in front of the restaurant his uncle Septemus.

Septemus was waving for James to cross the muddy street again.

Huddling into his soaked clothes, ready to feel the cold steady rain on his head and back again, James set forth across the swampy street.

4

In the night the Mexican prisoner and the white boy had taken a keen dislike to each other. Dodds was in the cell with the Mex kid trying to get him to talk about what had happened.

"I rolled over, and I fell out of bed," the Mex kid said. He looked over at the white boy and grinned.

The white boy had a narrow, feral face. He wore jail denims. He badly needed a shave but wouldn't accept the razor Dodds had several times tried to give him. He had eyes that were a mirror of all the things that had been done to him by others before he could defend himself, and all the things he wanted to do to people now that he was big and strong and dangerous. Once in a while Dodds felt sorry for kids like this but then he always reminded himself what a luxury such pity was. It had cost more than one lawman his life.

Dodds wanted the Mex to talk, but there he was intruding on the most sacred pact you found behind bars—no matter how much prisoners might hate each other, they hated a lawman more.

"I'd like to get this sonofabitch," Dodds said. "First because he snuck himself a knife into my jail. And second because he committed a felony while in my custody. That's the kind of thing that can really piss a man off."

"I don't know nothing about it. Nothing."

"What happens tonight?"

"Tonight?"

"Sure. When he gets another crack at you. Maybe you won't be so lucky tonight."

The white boy sat in the corner of his own cell, glaring first at Dodds then at the Mex kid.

For the first time, the Mex looked as if he just might believe what Dodds was saying.

The Mex raised his head and stared over at the white boy. "You s'posed to protect me while I'm in here."

"What the hell you think I'm *trying* to do?"

The Mex looked at the white boy again. "Let me think it over, okay?"

"Okay. But I wouldn't think about it much past sundown." Dodds grinned over at the white boy. "Not if you want to keep that punk off your back. He managed to stab you through the bars. That means he's got a good chance of killing you next time whether you're in separate cells or not."

"Sheriff," the deputy said through the barred door leading to the front office. "You got a visitor."

"Thanks," Dodds said, standing up. "If I ain't here, you give your statement to Eulo out there, okay?"

The Mex nodded.

The white boy grinned. Obviously he figured he had the Mex scared away.

Dodds hoped the Mex would surprise everybody and turn the white boy in. Assault with intent to commit great bodily injury would land the white boy in prison, where he belonged. All the white boy was doing time for was drunk and disorderly, but you could see that if somebody didn't stop him, he was the kind of kid who'd kill somebody for sure.

He started to make an obscene gesture behind Dodds's back at the sheriff headed for the front door.

Dodds turned around just in time to see what was about to happen. He grinned at the kid. That was one thing about punks. Mentally they never got much beyond second grade.

Dodds had always like Mae Kittredge. To some she was too religious, to others too strange, but she bore her disappointment over her lost child with a gentle dignity that touched Dodds. He remembered how Mae had helped the victims of the factory layoff, going door-to-door every few days to make sure that everyone had sufficient supplies of food and medicine, and sufficient supplies of tenderness for each other. Dodds had always joked to her that she'd make a fine sheriff; she could settle down riled-up husbands faster than any lawman he'd ever seen.

Now Mae sat in his office, her clothes damp from the rain. Her hands were folded in her lap, her eyes shaded by the bill of her bonnet. The way her lips moved softly, it was easy to tell she was praying.

Dodds came in and sat across from the desk and said, "Nice to see you, Mae."

As he said this, he realized he was going to be seeing a lot of the woman in the coming weeks. Her husband was, after all, implicated in a killing and a bank robbery.

"Nice to see you, Sheriff," she replied.

"How can I help you?"

"I just wanted to check up on that special deputy. After he left, I got suspicious."

"What deputy you talkin' about Mae?"

"The one who came out to the house. The one who works for the governor. The one who's helping you."

"My deputy's in back, Mae. He didn't go out to see you."

In her somber gray eyes came the realization that she'd been tricked.

"He asked about Dennis," she said.

"What about Dennis?"

"He wanted to know where he could find him."

"He say why?"

"He said Dennis had witnessed a jewelry robbery and he thought Dennis could testify against the robber."

"I see."

"It was a trick, wasn't it?'

He wanted to keep her calm. No reason to excite her. She'd had enough grief in recent years.

"I'm sure everything is fine, Mae," Dodds said, taking his pipe from his drawer. He stuck it between his teeth and inhaled it. He could taste the sweet and satisfying vapors of tobacco burned days ago. "He ask you where he could find Dennis?"

"He did."

"You tell him?"

"I did." Pause. "I shouldn't have, should I?"

He sucked a little more on his pipe. He tried to remain as composed as possible. The hell of it was he felt a little tic troubling the corner of his eye. He always got it when he got scared and he was scared now. Ryan was a crazy sonofabitch. Just in case he forgot how crazy, all he had to do was read the letter Ryan had written and left in his carpetbag. "Where'd you tell him he'd find Dennis, Mae?"

"Out on Lambert Creek. Up near Grovers Pass."

"Fishing, huh?"

"Umm-hmm."

This was the part he had to make sound really relaxed and nonchalant. "Why don't you let me do you a little favor, Mae?"

"A little favor?"

"Why don't you let me ride on out there and just see if I can find this fella. Ask him if there hasn't been some kind of mix-up or something."

She sighed. "I'd sure appreciate that, Sheriff."

"By the way, Mae, you haven't told me what this fella looks like exactly."

"Oh, he's a nice-looking man. You can tell he's successful and you can tell he's educated. He doesn't look like a criminal or anything."

"Could you be a little more specific, Mae? How tall he is and what color his hair is and what kind of clothes he's wearing."

She shrugged her narrow shoulders. "Sure, Sheriff. If you want me to."

The man she then proceeded to describe was, or course, Septemus Ryan.

5

The rain came hard enough to bother the bay that pulled the buggy. The animal spooked every so often on the mud road winding up through the clay hills.

James huddled back against the seat, trying to avoid getting any wetter than he already was. His clothes were still damp from trying to help Liz there in the street, and he hoped they would soon start to dry.

His uncle hied the horse and stared straight ahead. He leaned outside the protection of the top. Rain smashed against his skull and face but, if this bothered him, he didn't let James know it.

After a quarter mile, James said, "Where we going, Uncle Septemus?"

"You'll see." Septemus didn't turn around to address him.

"It's awful muddy."

"So it is."

"You're not worried about getting stuck?"

"The Lord is with us," Septemus said, speaking up so he could be heard over the downpour.

Then he hied the horse with the lash again and they sluiced through the gloom.

In forty-five minutes, Septemus and James came to the top of a draw. Through the rain James saw below, set between stands of white birch, a small cabin cut from hardwoods. The windows on either side of the door had been smashed and were stuffed with paper. There were no outbuildings except for a privy and no animals of any kind.

"We'll walk from here," Septemus said.

He jumped down, taking his Winchester with him, wrapping it inside his coat to protect it from the water.

"We're going down to the cabin?"

"Yes, we are."

They started walking.

"This the surprise you told me about?"

"Indeed it is, James. Indeed it is."

Septemus still wasn't looking at James. Instead he kept his gaze fixed on the cabin.

James knew he wasn't going to like the surprise. Something was wrong with Septemus and James knew that this meant the surprise would be something terrible. He kept thinking of what his uncle had said about responsibility. It had something to do with that.

When they reached the cabin, which smelled of wood and mildew in the rain, Septemus stood aside and waved James on to precede him.

James put his hand on the doorknob and said, "I'm not going to like this surprise, am I, Uncle Septemus?" Septemus shook his head. James had never seen him look this way before. So . . . strange. Rain dripped off the roof and fell onto James's head. "Am I?"

"You may not like it, James. But I know you'll fulfill your responsibility to Clarice anyway."

"To Clarice?"

"She was like your sister, wasn't she, James?

James knew how it would hurt Septemus if he denied this. "Yes, she was."

"Then you won't have any trouble doing your duty."

And with that, Septemus leaned forward and kicked the door inward. He kicked it hard enough that it slammed against the opposite wall. Dust rose up in the doorway and through the dust James saw a meanly furnished cabin with a cot that rats had eaten the straw out of, and a cast iron stove already rusting, and enough bent and dented cans of food to last a short winter.

But it was the man tied to the chair in the center of the one-room cabin that got James's attention.

You could see where the man had been badly beaten, his face discolored and his mouth raw with dried blood. There was a cut across his forehead and his left eye was blackened.

At first the man didn't speak—James wasn't certain he *could* speak, he looked so beaten up—he just stared at the two of them as they entered.

This was obviously the surprise, the man here, though what it meant exactly James wasn't yet sure.

Septemus said, "Do you know who this man is, James?"

"No," James said. "I don't."

"Run," the man said. "Run and get the law, kid. Get Sheriff Dodds." He strained against the bonds of rope that held him.

"He's one of the men who killed Clarice," Septemus said. "Kittredge."

"He's crazy, kid. Look at 'im. You can see it, can't you? That he's crazy?"

Septemus seemed not to have heard. "This is what I meant by responsibility, James. You've got to do what's right for Clarice."

"Kid, if I die, my wife won't have nobody. Nobody." The man looked as crazed with fear as Septemus did with anger.

James felt embarrassed for the man and had to drop his eyes. This was all so terrible; there was something unreal about it. It might almost have struck him as a nightmare except for the stink of the cabin itself and the raw look of the man's face. People just didn't have dreams that well detailed.

"Run, kid," the man said again.

Septemus held out the Winchester to James and said, "You take this, James, and you do right by Clarice. You hear me?"

James looked at the man in the chair. "Did you kill Clarice?"

The man looked miserable. "Kid, nobody killed the girl on purpose. It was an accident. We was out of work and couldn't find no jobs—that's the only reason we stuck up the bank in the first place."

The man was whining; again, James felt sorry for him.

"Why don't I go get the sheriff?" James said to his uncle.

"For what?"

"This man confessed, Uncle Septemus. All you have to do is turn him over. The law'll take care of it from that."

Septemus said, "You know why I brought you along on this trip?"

James knew better than to say anything.

"To learn how to be a man."

James hung his head.

"I show you one of the men who killed your cousin—the cousin who loved you—and what do you do? You talk about going to get the sheriff." Septemus waved the Winchester in the direction of Kittredge. "You're getting two things confused here, James. You're mistaking law for justice."

He walked over to Kittredge and stood next to him. Kittredge watched nervously. It was easy to see that Septemus wanted to start hitting him again.

Septemus said, "Now, in a court of law, Kittredge here might well convince a jury that Clarice's death was accidental. But we'd know better, wouldn't we, James? We'd know that that little girl would never have been killed if those men hadn't been there in the first place. Isn't that right, James?"

James nodded and glanced at Kittredge. Kittredge's eyes were huge and white, following Septemus around as the man paced.

"But being mature men, James—you and I—we won't settle

for law. We want justice. We want what's right." He raised the rifle. This time he didn't offer it to James, he merely held it out for James to see. "That's where personal responsibility enters into it, James. That's where you've got to act like a grown-up and do what's right."

This time he did hand James the Winchester.

Much as he didn't want to, James took the rifle in his hand and brought it close to his body.

"Kittredge is your turn. I've already killed Carlyle."

When Septemus said this, James felt a terrible chill come over him. "You killed a man, Uncle Septemus?"

"I most certainly did. One of the men who killed my Clarice. The same Clarice you yourself loved and cherished."

"Look at his face, kid," Kittredge said. "You can see he's crazy. Run and get the sheriff. Go on now before it's too late."

"You shouldn't have killed anybody," James said to his uncle, realizing abruptly what he'd been sensing ever since leaving Council Bluffs—that while this man might look like Septemus Ryan, he wasn't. No, there Kittredge was right. This was an insane man who bore only a passing resemblance to his uncle.

Septemus said, nodding to the Winchester, "Raise the rifle and sight it, James. Just like I showed you when you were a boy. Raise the rifle and sight it and do your duty."

"Go run and get the sheriff, kid. Hurry."

"You going to listen to the man who killed your Clarice, James? Now raise that rifle and sight it and make Clarice proud."

"Please, son. Please don't listen to him. He's insane. He already killed one man and he'll surely kill me."

"James, don't let me down. Now raise that rifle and sight it and do what's right."

"Please, son."

"Raise the rifle, James."

And James—looking at Septemus, loving Septemus and knowing his uncle's relentless grief and agony ever since the death of his daughter—James raised the rifle into a firing position.

"That's a good boy, James. Now sight it, just like I always showed you."

Squinting, James sighted along the barrel. All he could think of was that maybe Septemus was right. Maybe he wasn't being a man. Maybe he did owe it to Clarice. Maybe the only way he was ever really going to grow up and have the respect of others, let alone the respect of himself, was to pull the trigger on the man who'd helped kill Clarice. James thought of his little cousin, how sweet and gentle she'd been, and how both his aunt and uncle had been destroyed by her death.

"Kid, I ain't got this coming. I really ain't," Kittredge said. "Please, kid."

Kittredge started crying.

James sighted the rifle.

"Make me proud of you, James," Uncle Septemus said. "Make Clarice proud."

Kittredge had closed his eyes, waiting for death.

James said, "I can't do it."

"You can do it, son. Just relax. You can do it fine."

"You'll be a killer if you do it, kid. You'll be a killer and they'll put you in prison."

"You just relax, James. You can do it fine."

James said, "I can't do it, I really can't. It isn't right."

Septemus slapped James harder than James had ever been slapped before. A terrible hot feeling filled James's face, and his head spun with stars.

"Now you get up there, James," Septemus said. "You get up there and do your responsibility."

Kittredge said, "You know what's right, kid. Don't give in to him. If you do you'll be just as crazy as he is. You know what we done was an accident, don't you kid?"

Septemus took James by the shoulder and turned him around so he was again facing Kittredge. He took the rifle and moved it into a firing position in James' hands.

"Now don't waste any more time, James. Shoot."

"Kid, listen, please—"

"Shoot!"

Their voices filling his head, the dank stink of the cabin filling his nose, the pathetic and somehow irritating spectacle of a man pleading for his life filling his mind—James let the Winchester slip from his hands to the floor.

He turned and ran from the cabin.

He went outside, just out from under the overhang, so he could stand in the rain, and the sound of it would drown out the madness of his uncle and the mewling of Kittredge who had, after all, been at least partly responsible for Clarice's death.

The rain came down silver and seemed to cleanse him and he put his hands out and opened his mouth to receive it, letting the drops splat on his face and trickle down his neck and soak into his coat.

Then, even through the snapping rain, he heard it, the gunshot, and knew what had happened.

He didn't feel any regret for Kittredge; the regret was for his uncle. There would be no way back now.

He turned and stood in the rain and after a few minutes Septemus came out of the cabin.

Septemus came a few feet up the slope of the hill. He didn't seem to notice the rain soaking him.

"You let me down, James."

"I know."

"I always considered you like a son. Loved you in that same way."

"Just the way I loved you, Uncle Septemus."

"But when the time came to prove how much you loved me and loved my Clarice—" He fell silent. Rain pocked the summer-brown grass and drummed against the cabin roof. Blue-gray gunsmoke wafted out the cabin door. You could smell the blood of an animal kill on the air. In this case the animal had been human.

"You should let me help you, Uncle Septemus."

"I don't want anything more to do with you, James. Your mother has not raised you to be a man and it's too late now for me to do anything about it."

"I don't want them to hurt you, Uncle Septemus. That's why I wish you'd give me the rifle and let me take you into town."

Septemus raised his head in the rain and looked directly at James. "I know what the dead men say."

"What?"

"I know what the dead men say. They whisper to me, James. They tell me secrets. They reassure me. This"—he waved his arms in a patriarchal way to indicate the land and the cliffs surrounding them—"none of this is what it seems, James. Even Clarice tells me that when she talks to me."

"There's one more, isn't there?"

Through the beating rain, Septemus studied him. "Are you thinking of redeeming yourself with Griff, with the last one?" He waggled the rifle in James's direction. "Are you saying that you want to take this Winchester and do what's right?"

"I'm saying that you should leave him be. Killing two men is enough."

For a time, only the rain made sound. It seemed to be saying something, its hissing and pounding and spattering a language James yearned to understand, a dialogue shared only by rock and soil and leaves and grass.

"He has two daughters."

"Who?"

"The last one," Septemus said.

"They didn't kill Clarice."

"I want him to know how it feels."

The rain continued to speak.

James said, "Please give me your rifle, Uncle Septemus. Please let me take you in. They won't blame you for what you did. They'll understand."

"I'm going now, James."

Septemus started up the hill. "Please let me help you, Uncle Septemus!"

110

James slipped and fell on the wet grass. Septemus walked on ahead, never once looking back.

Scrambling to his feet, James went up the hill again, trying to grab his uncle's sleeve.

"Please, Uncle Septemus, please—"

With no hesitation, Septemus turned around and doubled his fist and hit James square on the jaw.

James felt as if he'd been shot. He saw darkness and felt a rush of cold air go up his nose and sinuses. He felt himself fall back and slam against the soggy earth. And for a moment then there was nothing at all, just a horrible spinning that made him nauseous and an overwhelming pain in the lower part of his face. He wondered if his uncle had broken his jaw.

Then, on the hill, there was the clop of hooves and the creaking of the buggy. Septemus hied the horse.

Septemus was gone.

He wasn't sure how long he lay there.

The rain soaked him, running into his eyes, his mouth, his nose.

Sometime during the darkness, before he had quite recovered his senses, he heard a horse on the road above. Then he heard a man, breathing hard and cursing under his breath, move carefully down the hill that was by now a mudslide.

When he opened his eyes, he saw Dodds peering down at him. "You all right, boy?"

"He hit me."

"Who?"

"My uncle Septemus."

"Where is he now?"

"I don't know."

"What happened?"

"You'd better look in the cabin."

"What's in the cabin?"

"Just go look."

While Dodds was gone, James struggled to his feet. He felt as if he would never be dry again. He had heard stories of Indians leaving white men out in downpours and by so doing drove them insane. James could see how that would be possible.

He had taken two steps down the hill when Dodds came out of the cabin.

"He did that, didn't he, your uncle."

"Yes."

"The crazy sonofabitch."

"That's his problem, Sheriff. He's crazy. Crazy over his girl dying. He said that that was one of the men who did it." He hesitated. "He killed another one, too. At least that's what he said."

"He tell you the name?"

"Carlyle."

"God damn it." Dodds said. "I've got to stop him." He looked back at the cabin. The rain hit him steady on the back of his balding head. "He was a pretty decent man, Kittredge was." He turned back to James. "It's sure as hell none of those men killed that little girl on purpose. Not even Carlyle. He was a lout but not a killer. Not of little girls, leastwise."

"That's why he's going to Griff's," he said.

"Why?"

"Because Griff has two little girls of his own."

Dodds stared at him. "You may have to help me, son. You willing?"

"He's my uncle."

"I know that."

"And I love him. He's pretty much been my father since my real father died."

Dodds nodded to the cabin. "You should go back in there and take a look at Kittredge."

James gulped. "I don't want to."

"He shot him in the face. Dead on. You ever seen that before?"

"No."

"Well, believe me, son, it's nothing to see."

"You aren't going to shoot him, are you?"

"Not unless I have to."

"Let me talk to him, then."

"Long as he don't hurt nobody else, talking to him is fine. I can't tell you what I'm going to feel like if he hurts either of those little girls."

"I feel sorry for him."

"I feel sorry for him, too, son. But I feel a hell of a lot sorrier for those girls."

Dodds started up the hill. "We're gonna have to ride double, so we better get goin'. That poor old horse of mine ain't that fast anymore."

As he made his way carefully up the hill, James said again, "You promise me you won't shoot him, Sheriff?"

Dodds looked back at him and said, "It's a little late for promises of any kind, son. We're just gonna have to see what happens."

Chapter Seven

1

He stood beneath a dripping oak, feeling tired suddenly, older than he ever had.

An early dusk gave the rain an even colder feel now, and put lights on in the windows of the small white houses on the small respectable street where Griff and his family lived.

He could see Griff in the window now, bending to turn up the wick in a kerosene lamp. He wondered if Griff had any sense that his two companions were dead.

Septemus Ryan hefted the Winchester and started walking down the block to where the alley began. Getting into Griff's house would not be easy. Going in through the rear would probably be best.

He passed picket fences and flower beds, neatly trimmed shrubs and tidy green lawns.

Griff's barn dominated the alley. The other buildings were small white garages. He did not have to worry about being seen because it had been raining so long and so steadily that nobody would be looking out the window. Or so he told himself.

As he strode over the wet cinders of the alley, he heard the voices, faintly. There was Clarice, thanking him for his brave actions today. And then the chorus of dead men—relatives and friends who'd gone on before—telling him that they were waiting for him, that the other side was good and he would like it and there was nothing to fear.

An uncle spoke to him, and then a brother dead early of consumption, and then a schoolmate killed in the war, and then an old muttonchopped mentor who'd advised him in the ways of business . . .

All these people whispered to Septemus Ryan, and said that Clarice was with them, and that like them, she awaited sight of her father as he crossed over.

And as he walked, there in the rain, the unrelenting hissing rain a curtain that lent everything a spectral cast, he had the sense that he was already walking the land of the dead, all humanity fading, fading behind the curtain of rain, alone in a curious and endless realm of phantoms and whispered voices.

He reached the barn and went in through the back door. He stood in the center of the dark, dusty place smelling the hay and the lubricating oils Griff used on his buggies and the sweet tart tang of horseshit from the stall where they kept the gelding.

He felt tired again, exhausted.

He looked enviously at the gelding. He wanted to go over and lay down next to it in the straw and hay, share the colorful threadbare horse blanket, and sleep with his arm thrown across the fleshy warm side of the animal, the way he'd once slept with his wife.

He went to the front sliding door and stood watching the rain fall in big silver drops from the roof. He could see nightcrawlers and worms swimming in the clear puddles around his feet; he could smell rusted iron tangy from the rain; he could see mist rising like ghosts from the slanting roof of the Griff house, and hear faintly, the way he once heard Clarice, the clear pure laughter of a little girl.

I remember you sleeping between your mother and I remember your soft pink cheeks so warm when you kissed me your eyes so lovely and blue how you made little snoring sounds in the middle of the night and kept your doll pulled so tight to you.

He saw her in the window now, just her head, the little girl.

He hefted his Winchester and started across the soggy grass.

There was a screened-in back porch with chairs for sitting. He eased open the back door and went inside. He could smell dampness on the stone floor and dinner from the kitchen just behind the door. It smelled good and warm and he realized how hungry he was.

There were no voices. From his glimpse in the window a minute ago he'd been able to see that the little girl was probably alone in the kitchen. That would make it easier.

We used to swing till dark in the summertime on the rope swing in the backyard, your hair shining gold even in the dusk and the firefly darkness and your mother calling lemonade's ready, lemonade's ready and the way you'd giggle and writhe as I'd tickle you on the way inside and your mother and I reading to you in the lampglow of your room as you fell asleep.

The door was open.

He went up two steps and found himself in the kitchen. It was about what he'd expected, modest but quite orderly. A girl of six or seven stood at the sink, drying dishes and then stacking them neatly on the sideboard.

He went straight up to her.

Just as she heard him, just as she started to turn to see what the noise was, he brought his hand around to the front of her face and covered her mouth.

With the other hand, he put the Winchester to her head.

"I want you to call out for your papa, you understand?"

Against the palm of his hand, he could feel the girl's hot breath and her saliva and the tiny edges of her teeth.

The girl nodded.

"Go ahead now," he said.

Before she called out, the girl twisted her neck so she could get a quick glimpse of him.

She looked terrified.

She said, "Papa. It's Eloise. Could you come out here, please?"

"Couldn't I finish my pipe first, hon?" he said.

Ryan nudged the little girl.

"I need you to come here now, Papa."

This time when she talked her voice broke with tension.

This time her papa came right away.

He came to the doorway of the kitchen and saw them.

He surprised Ryan by not saying anything.

He just stood there gawking, as if he could not believe it.

Finally, Griff said, "She doesn't have any part in this."

By now, his wife, apparently curious, came to the kitchen doorway, too.

She immediately made a noise that resembled mewling. "Oh, Eloise," she said.

"She doesn't have any part in this," Griff said again.

"My little girl didn't have any part in your robbery, either."

"Please, mister, please let her go," Griff's wife said.

Her mother's tone was scaring the girl even more. She strained against Ryan's hard grasp.

"I'm taking her," Ryan said.

"Oh, no!" her mother said and tried to lunge through the door to take her daughter.

Her husband put out a strong arm and stopped her. He said, "Go in the other room and make sure Tess is all right. I'll take care of this."

"Why would he want Eloise?" the woman said. She was becoming so distraught she sounded crazed.

"Go take care of Tess," he said.

Then, his wife gone, Griff said, "Take me, Ryan. You let Eloise walk over to me and you can take me anywhere you want. And do whatever you want. Just don't take it out on my daughter, you understand?"

Helping you with your homework at the dining room table how you always had the tiny pink corner of your tongue sticking out of your mouth when you were stumped by a problem and how you always had ink stains on the index finger of your right hand and worried that boys wouldn't think you were pretty because of the stains.

Ryan said, "I wanted you to know that I'm taking her. I wanted you to see it, Griff. To fear for it."

Eloise started crying.

Griff said, "I'm sorry for what happened to your daughter, Ryan."

It was then that he dived across the small kitchen to try and snatch Eloise away from Ryan, and it was then that Ryan shot Griff—two quick explosions of the Winchester—directly in the arm and leg.

2

Half a mile from town, the horse James and Dodds rode began to give out. He not only slowed, his legs were unsteady in the mud.

Dodds reined him in at a tree and said, "We'd better go on foot from here."

In the rain the horse looked cold and sick, his hazel eyes glazed, ragged breath rocking his ribs every few seconds.

Dodds saw how James was watching the horse over his shoulder as the two set off walking fast for town.

"Don't worry, son," Dodds said. "He just has the same problem I do."

"What problem's that?"

"Same problem you'll have and your own son'll have. Age. He's just old and the rain's got him spooked a little. I'll come back for him in a while and put him up in the livery and hay him and rub him down and he'll be fine."

"He's a nice horse."

"You get real attached to things, don't you, son?"

James shrugged, wiping rain from his face. He had been out in the downpour so long that he knew it would feel odd when the rain stopped. Human beings seemed to get used to things, even things they basically didn't like. "I guess I do."

As they walked, Dodds looked over at him and said, "I want to tell you something."

"What?"

"That I'll do my best not to shoot him."

"I appreciate that, Sheriff."

"I just hope he doesn't back me into a corner."

"People do that to you?"

"All the time. They get distraught or they get drunk or they get heartbroke and then they do very foolish things and they don't leave me much leeway."

"I'll talk to Septemus. He'll listen to me."

"I hope so, son. I hope so."

3

Dora got bandages and worked on her husband's arm and leg. There was a lot of blood. The first thing the two girls had done was scream. The second thing they did was start crying. Now they were silent, just watching it, how their mother was on her knees patching up their father, how Ryan just stood there with his Winchester.

"You shouldn't have shot him, mister," the wife said.

"He shouldn't have shot my daughter."

She just shook her head, looked at her husband's wounds again. Griff had his eyes closed. He'd tried to stand up several times but his wife wouldn't let him. He lay on the kitchen floor now with his head propped on three dishtowels she'd rolled up for a pillow.

Tess, the youngest girl, said, "I don't like you."

Ryan said, "Well, I like you. I like all little girls. Every single one of them."

"You hurt my papa."

"Well, he hurt somebody I cared about very much."

"Who?"

"My own little girl."

"Tess get over here," her mother said.

"How come Eloise can't come over with us?"

Her mother said, "The man won't let her."

"How come?"

"Get over here, Tess."

"My papa didn't hurt nobody," Tess said, and then kind of ambled over to stand next to her mother.

Ryan gripped Eloise's shoulder tight again and said, "I'm going to walk out of here with her now, ma'm."

"No!"

The woman jumped to her feet.

Her husband's eyes opened and the man tried to struggle to his feet. This time his wife didn't stop him.

Tess, sensing all the alarm, started sobbing. "What's he going to do, Mama?"

"Be quiet." The woman glared at Ryan. "No matter what happened, mister, my daughter don't deserve to be treated like this."

"Neither did my daughter."

"You let her go, you bad man," Tess said.

Griff had now managed to get himself upright. He was white from loss of blood and pasty-looking. His eyes didn't quite focus.

There was blood all over his clothes. "I told you, Ryan. Take me. I'm the one you want."

"No, Griff. This will be worse. Taking your daughter. Then you'll know what I've been going through."

And with that, he picked the girl up and tucked her under his arm. He was strong enough to hold her even when she wriggled. He backed out of the kitchen to the stairs.

To the woman he said, "I'm sorry about this, ma'm. But it's the only way."

Eloise started screaming.

Ryan got one step down the back stairs and then two steps and then he moved quickly out the door.

4

By the time James and Dodds reached the alley that ran behind the Griff house, they could hear shouts and screams even above the rain.

"He's there," Dodds said, pulling his Navy Colt from his holster.

"You said you weren't going to shoot him," James said, panic filling his chest.

"Son, I said I'd try not to shoot him. But I didn't say I'd be foolish. He'll be armed and so will I." He nodded to a small garage to their left. "You could always go in there and stay till it's over."

"I want to go with you. I want to talk to him."

"All right," Dodds said, "c'mon, then."

They went up the alley. Even the cinders were squishy underfoot.

A hundred feet away they saw Septemus come into the alley, Eloise Griff pulled close to him, the Winchester not far from her head.

Dodds shouted, "Stop right there, Ryan."

Dodds and James started running toward the man and the little girl.

Around the corner of the barn came Mrs. Griff and her husband.

Griff was crudely bandaged; blood soaked through several places in his shirt and trousers. He looked as if he were about ready to collapse.

Mrs. Griff was slowly, painfully pleading with Ryan to let her little girl go.

When Dodds and James reached them, Dodds walked as close to Ryan as Septemus would let him.

Ryan put the muzzle of the Winchester directly against Eloise's head. "I'm going to kill her, Sheriff. Stand back."

James stared at the man who'd once been his uncle. This impostor bore no resemblance. "Uncle Septemus," he said.

As if recognizing his presence for the first time, Septemus glanced over at him and shook his head. For a brief moment there, he did resemble the old Septemus. Concern filled his eyes. "You shouldn't have come, James. I shouldn't have brought you along. It was a mistake. You shouldn't have anything to do with this."

"Uncle Septemus, you can't kill that little girl," James said, stepping up closer to Dodds.

All of them stood there in the rain, cold now and soaking but unable to take their eyes from the man and the girl.

"I know what I have to do, James. I have to make things right. I'm sorry, this is the only way I can do it." Septemus pulled the girl tighter to him. "Now stand back, James. Stand back."

"Please, Sheriff, talk to him," Mrs. Griff said. One could hear how hard she was working at keeping herself sane, fighting against the impulse to be hysterical.

"Ryan," Dodds said, advancing another step or two. "Hand me the Winchester and let the little girl go."

"Don't make me shoot you, Sheriff," Septemus said. "I've got nothing against you. This is between Griff and me."

Griff hobbled up closer himself. "Just take me, Ryan. Just take me and let Eloise walk away."

Dodds, seeing that Ryan was momentarily watching Griff talk, took another step.

Ryan lowered the Winchester and shot him in the shoulder.

Dodds flailed, pieces of his shirt and his shoulder exploding. He went over backward and lay in a puddle in the middle of the alley.

Mrs. Griff went to him much as she'd done with her husband. She had his head up against her forearm. Dodds's eyes were open and he was saying something to Mrs. Griff in a slow, small voice. James couldn't hear them. Now all he could hear was the rain; the rain.

As James turned back to Septemus, he noticed the Navy Colt that Dodds had dropped.

Impulsively, he bent and picked it up.

Septemus watched him.

When James turned back to his uncle, he held the Navy Colt.

"You go on, now, James," Septemus said. "You go to the depot and get a train back to Council Bluffs."

"I want you to let the little girl go," James said.

He stood ten feet from his uncle, the Colt in his hand.

"Put the gun down," Septemus said.

"Uncle Septemus, you can't see yourself. You can't know how you look and sound. I know how much you loved Clarice but this isn't right. Not with this little girl."

Septemus looked down at Eloise a moment. His grip seemed to loosen.

"Please, Uncle Septemus," James said. "Please, let her go."

To his right, James could see the Griff woman saying a silent prayer that Septemus would just let the girl walk away.

Septemus's grip let up considerably now.

James could see Eloise start to slip away.

"No!" Septemus shouted.

It was as if some spell had come over him suddenly. He was no longer James's uncle but the crazed, ugly man he'd been a few minutes ago; the one that he'd been back at the cabin where he'd killed Dennis Kittredge.

He grabbed the girl and jerked her back to him and slammed the Winchester against her temple once again.

James started walking toward Septemus, the Colt level in his hand. He wasn't even sure he could fire it properly. At this point he didn't care. Now that he knew how insane Septemus had become, all James could think of was freeing the little girl. He loved the man who'd been his uncle too much to do anything else.

"Let her go, Uncle Septemus," James said, advancing.

"I'll shoot you, James," Septemus said. "Don't think I won't."

Two, three, four more steps.

"Let her go, Uncle Septemus."

"You heard me, James."

Five, six, seven more steps.

"Let her go, Uncle Septemus."

"Please, James; please don't come any closer."

Septemus pulled the Winchester from the little girl and leveled it directly at James.

James dived then, not knowing if his uncle would fire or not; dived directly for the little girl.

He slammed into them hard enough that Septemus's grip on the girl's shoulder was broken.

"Run!" James shouted to her.

Eloise ran, stumbling across the cinders and puddles.

Her mother ran out to swoop her up.

By now, James was flat on the ground.

Septemus had run into the darkness of the barn. He stood in the shadows, holding the Winchester at his side.

James got to his feet, picking up the Colt again. He felt an idiotic happiness that Septemus was still alive.

Dodds saw what James was about to do. Still lying on the ground, Dodds raised a hand and said, "Don't you go in there, son. Wait till some deputies get here."

But James didn't listen.

He went through the barn door. Rain dripped and plopped off the door into the silver puddles.

Septemus stood in the shadows.

He said, "I'm glad I didn't kill that little girl."

He started crying then.

James had never heard sounds so terrible.

After he had sobbed for a time, Septemus raised his head and said, "Do you love me, James?"

"You know I do, Uncle Septemus."

"Then will you help me?"

"I'll do anything you want me to, Uncle Septemus."

"You know what they'll do to me. The trial and all. It won't be good for anybody. You know what something like that would do to your mother."

"She loves you, too, Uncle Septemus. She knows how Clarice's death affected you."

"Raise that Colt, James."

"What?"

"Raise that Colt and shoot me."

"Uncle Septemus—"

Septemus shook his head. "It'll be better for everybody, James. You can see what all this has done to me. I'm not a killer, James, yet I've killed two men and I almost killed a little girl. I don't want to live anymore, James, yet I'm not sure I can take my own life because I'm afraid I'd be damned to hell."

"Uncle Septemus, I couldn't do that. I couldn't."

"I can hear her, James. Clarice, I mean. I want to be with her again. I want to hold her in my arms and sing to her and tell her how much I love her." Then his eyes in the gloom took on the clarity of the insane; that terrible vivid truth that only they can see. "Take the Colt, James. And do it. You'll be helping everybody."

"I can't."

"Just raise it up to my chest, James."

"I don't want to, Uncle Septemus."

"It's your duty, James. I was wrong about you helping me kill the others. But this time I'm not wrong, James. You need to grow and take the responsibility for the whole family, James."

"He's right, son; it'll be better this way."

From the door, Dodds hobbled inside. The blood on his shoulder was faded from the rain. His scratchy, wavery voice told how weak the gunshot had left him.

When Ryan saw him, he said, "I'm sorry I shot you, Sheriff."

"I know, Mr. Ryan. I don't hold you accountable. Not really." Dodds looked at James. "I'm going to get some deputies, son, so we can take Mr. Ryan into custody and so I can get somebody to do something about my shoulder. But I want to tell you something."

James shook his head. "I don't want to do it, sir."

Dodds said, "He's right about it, son. It'll be better for everybody. He can't help the way he is now and about the only thing we can do for him is to get him out of his misery." Dodds nodded to the door. "I'm going to walk out of here and I won't have any idea what happens. If your uncle gets shot and you tell me it was self-defense, then I'm just going to have to take your word for it, won't I, son?"

Dodds looked at Septemus then. "I'm sorry about your little girl, Mr. Ryan."

He left the barn.

They stood alone facing each other. In the stall in the back they could hear the horse get restless with nightfall.

Somewhere beyond the rain there would be stars and the vast darkness of night. James just wanted to be a boy and sit in his bedroom window and dream idly about all the mysteries of the universe.

He did not want to be standing in a barn smelling of hay and horseshit and oil and facing his uncle in this way.

"You've got to help me, James," Septemus said, and fell to crying once more.

But this time he let the Winchester fall from his hands and he came over to James and embraced him.

James had never heard or felt this kind of grief before. His uncle's sobbing was too painful for either of them to abide for long.

"Help me, James; help me," Uncle Septemus said, leaning back from the boy.

Septemus took the barrel of the Colt and raised it to his chest and said, "Please help me, James. Please help me."

"Uncle Septemus—"

"Please, James."

James shot twice, the first shot not seeming to do anything, Septemus just hovering there, his face that of a stranger again.

With the second shot, however, Septemus fell to the ground on his back.

He looked up at James. "Thank you, James. You did your duty."

Then it was James who began to cry, wild with grief and fear, filled with disbelief that he might have done such a thing.

"Uncle Septemus!" he cried.

But it was too late.

Septemus's eyes had closed. In death he was himself again, the lines of his face softer, gentleness joining the intelligence of his brow.

"Uncle Septemus!" James cried out again.

But only the horse in the back was there to hear.

James rose then and went to the barn door and looked out through the rain. In the distance he could hear the slapping footsteps of men running. In the gloom their shouts were ugly and harsh. The deputies.

He felt so many things, and yet he felt nothing. He thought of his mother and Marietta and Liz; he thought of his dead cousin Clarice and the sound of the gunshot back there at the cabin where Kittredge had died; and he thought finally of Septemus, of the terrible things that can happen to human beings and of the terrible things those very same human beings are then capable of visiting on others.

If this was being a man, perhaps he didn't want to be a man. Maybe it was better to be a dreamy boy, passing by Marietta's house on a night of fireflies and banjos, her idle flirtations making him happier than he'd ever been before.

But something had changed in him now; and no matter how much he yearned to be the boy he'd been, he knew he could never be that boy again. He possessed some terrible knowledge now, some insight that would stay with him forever like a curse.

Then the men were there, the deputies, and the air was filled with the harsh barking curses of men who tried to convince themselves and each other that they were in control of things.

5

"You sure you don't want to do anything? You already paid, you know."

"I just want to lie here."

"In the darkness?"

"Yes."

"Till it's time for your train?"

"Yes."

Liz said, "You seem very different from last night."

He said nothing.

"I'm sorry about your uncle."

"I know."

She paused. "I'd like to kiss you, James."

He said nothing.

"I'd like to kiss you like a friend, James. Like somebody who cares about you very much."

She kissed him. He held her there a long time. He liked the warmth of her body against his. In the room next door a man laughed and his whore giggled.

"You shouldn't stay here a lot longer," James said.

"I been thinking that myself lately."

"Do you s'pose you'll really do it? Get out of here, I mean?"

She said, "I sure like to think so, James. I sure like to think so."

The train was a Chicago, Milwaukee, and St. Paul. A Short Line with Pullman sleepers and a long dining car.

James got a seat and the train rumbled away and was then hurtling through the vast prairie night. The rain had stopped and there was a hazy moon out now, casting silver on the cornfields and wheatfields and the cows in silhouette on the distant hills.

And James sat there alone, no longer James, not the old James anyway, but somebody else now, somebody he was not even sure he liked at all.